FULL COLOR

CAPTAIN UNDERPANTS

AND THE TERRIFYING RE-TURN OF TIPPY TINKLETROUSERS

The Ninth Epic Novel by

DAV PILKEY

with color by Jose Garibaldi
and Wes Dzioba

Scholastic Inc.

Library of Congress Control Number: 2018959190
ISBN 978-1-338-34721-0

10 9 8 7 6 5 4 3 2 1   19 20 21 22 23

Cover design by Dav Pilkey and Phil Falco
Book design by Dav Pilkey, Kathleen Westray, and Phil Falco
Color by Jose Garibaldi and Wes Dzioba

Printed in China   62
First color edition printing, December 2019

For Aaron Mancini

CHAPTERS

FOREWORD:
The Supa Top-Secret Truth About Captain Underpants   7

1. George and Harold   13
2. The Banana Cream Pie Paradox   19
3. The Real Ending to Our Last Adventure   27
4. Life in the Big House   31
5. The Unveiling   39
6. Calling Captain Underpants   50
7. Tippy's Trouser Troubles   59
8. Break in Two: Electric Boogaloo   68
9. Exactly Five Years, Eleven Days,
   Fourteen Hours, and Six Minutes Ago . . .   73
10. Meet George   86
11. Furious George   92
12. The Incredibly Graphic Violence Chapter
    (in Flip-O-Rama™)   99
13. The Detention   114
14. The Adventures of Dog Man   121
15. The Plan   137
16. Super Spies   143
17. Monday   150
18. Things Get Ugly   163

19. Who Is Wedgie Magee? 170

20. Tuesday Afternoon 179

21. Things Get Even Uglier 182

22. Wednesday 186

23. Thursday 193

24. Foamy, White Ectoplasm 201

25. Thursday Afternoon 213

26. When Kipper Gets Angry—
    Really, Really Angry 219

27. Something Wedgie This Way Comes 229

28. The Curse of Wedgie Magee (A True Story) 239

29. The Perfect Storm 251

30. The Wonderful, Happy, Incredibly
    Delightful Ending 268

31. The Terrible, Sad, Incredibly
    Horrifying Ending 277

32. Four Years Later . . . 289

33. To Make a Long Story Short 296

34. The End (of the World as We Know It) 298

THE SUPA TOP SECRET TRUTH ABOUT CAPTAIN UNDER-PANTS

BY George and Harold

Onse upon a while ago, there was two cool kids named George and Harold.

We da Bomb Pops!

me too!

They had a rilly mean principle named Mr. Krupp.

BLah BLaH BLah and stuff!

So they Hipnitized Him.

YOU WiLL obey us!

OK!

You are now Captain Underpants!

groovy!

Mr. Krupp rilly thout He WAS captain underpants...

tra-La-Laaaa!

... and He got in lots of trubble!!!

One time Dr. Diaper Kidnapped him...

Haw Haw Haw!

... and George and Harold had to save him.

Boo-ya!

Bye Bye!

I'm Free!

rats!

Another time He almost got ate up by some talking Toilets...

Yum Yum eat em up!

... and George and Harold had to save him again!!!

EAT this!

Cafateria Food

I'm a Hero!

and then this other time a buncha **ZOMBIE** nerds atacked.

Captain Under-
pants dranked
Some super
Power JUISE

and He got
Supa Powers!

Then He saved
George and
Harold.

HERES the worst part...

whenever mr.
KRUPP Hears
somebody snap
their fingers...

Blah
Blah Blah

snap

He Turns
into capta-
in underpan-
ts!

Tra
La-
Laaa!

And whenever
captain Under-
pants gets water
on his head...

splash!

He Turns
Back into
mr. KRUPP!

Blah Blah
BLaH!!!!!

So whatever you do, dont snap your fingers at mr. krupp!!!

seriousley, dudes!

Ixnay on the napping-say!!!

↑ pig Laten

and if you ever see captain underpants saving the world, Hide the H2O!!!

POW

QUICK!!!! NOBODY pour water on his head!!!

Tree House comix ink.

CHAPTER 1
GEORGE AND HAROLD

This is George Beard and Harold Hutchins. George is the kid on the right with the tie and the flat-top. Harold is the one on the left with the T-shirt and the bad haircut. Remember that now.

When our last adventure ended, George and Harold were being escorted to jail. The police had discovered surveillance photos showing the two boys robbing a bank with Captain Underpants. Of course, we all know that George, Harold, and Captain Underpants were innocent. It was their *evil twins* who had robbed that bank. But the police hadn't bothered to read the last book, so they really didn't know what was going on.

All they knew was that George and Harold *looked* a lot like the two kids in the surveillance photos. So the cops yelled *"FREEZE!"* and grabbed George and Harold, then told the two boys of their terrible fate.

Suddenly, a gigantic pair of robotic pants
appeared from out of nowhere. The terrifying
Tippy Tinkletrousers emerged from the
zipper, zapped the cops with an ice ray . . .

. . . and chased George and Harold (and their two pets, Crackers and Sulu) far into the cavernous depths of the lower right-hand corner of page 17.

If you read our last epic novel, you know that this is how the story ended. But that's not how it was *supposed* to end.

You see, Tippy and his giant ice-ray-zapping robotic trousers weren't supposed to be there at all. They had come from the future and rudely interrupted what was *supposed* to happen.

Unfortunately for Tippy, the simple act of sending himself backward through time would end up being a terrible, terrible mistake. A mistake that would ultimately lead to the destruction of our entire planet, more or less.

But before I can tell you that story, I have to tell you *this* story . . .

CHAPTER 2
THE BANANA CREAM PIE PARADOX

Time machines are awesome. There's no doubt about it. But they can also be very dangerous. It's possible that a person could go back in time and accidentally change one little thing—and that one teeny, tiny, itsy-bitsy thing could profoundly affect the future. This is what scientists refer to as the *Banana Cream Pie Paradox*.

THE BANANA CREAM PIE PARADOX

PLEASE FOLLOW ALONG WITH THESE HANDY ILLUSTRATIONS

Imagine, if you will, that a scientist from the year 2020 baked a banana cream pie using bananas that he harvested from his very own banana tree.

Let's suppose now that this scientist took his banana cream pie into a time machine, which zapped him (and the pie) back to the year 1936.

Now imagine that the scientist stepped out of his time machine and accidentally tripped, smashing his pie into the face of a lady sitting at a fancy garden party.

Now suppose that the lady
jumped up angrily, wiped
a handful of gooey banana
cream pie filling from her
face, and threw it at
the scientist.

The scientist ducked . . .

. . . causing the banana goo to smack into
the face of a gentleman standing nearby.

A waitress pointed
at the gentleman
and laughed.

The angry gentleman
wiped the goo from
his face . . .

. . . and smooshed it into
the waitress's face.

"Well!" said the waitress.
"I've never been so
insulted in all my life!"

"You oughtta get out more, lady!
N'yuk, n'yuk, n'yuk!" said a wise guy.

"Why don't you mind your own business,
birdbrain?" said another man . . .

. . . as he poked
the wise guy
in the eyes.

The wise guy fell
backward and landed
on the scientist's banana
tree (which was just a
tiny sapling in 1936).

The tiny banana tree
snapped in half
and died.

Now, if the scientist's banana tree died in 1936, it could never grow up and produce bananas.

Therefore, the scientist would not have had the main ingredient he used to make his banana cream pie in the year 2020.

Consequently, the banana cream pie could not exist.

TELL THAT
TO *THESE* GUYS!

Many scientists throughout the centuries have pondered the Banana Cream Pie Paradox and have come to the conclusion that people should be really, really, really, REALLY, *REALLY* careful when they use time machines. Because one simple change in the past could affect the future . . . and even possibly destroy our entire planet.

CHAPTER 3
THE REAL ENDING TO OUR LAST ADVENTURE

As we already saw in chapter 1, George and Harold were being taken to jail when Tippy Tinkletrousers traveled backward through time and interfered. But what would have happened if he hadn't showed up? What was *supposed* to happen (before Tippy so rudely interrupted them)? Well, sit back and get comfortable, because you're about to find out!

The Police Chief and his right-hand man, Officer McWiggly, handcuffed George and Harold and shuffled them into the back of their police car.

"You've got the wrong guys," cried Harold. "We didn't rob that bank!"

"It's true," said George. "That bank was robbed by our evil twins from an alternate universe!"

"Yeah, *right*," said Officer McWiggly. "If I had a nickel for every time I've heard *THAT* excuse!"

On the way to jail, the cops drove past Mr. Krupp, who was busy cleaning up the soggy toilet paper in his yard.

"Hey!" shouted the Police Chief. "That's the guy who robbed the bank with those kids!"

"Let's get him!" yelled Officer McWiggly.

29

★ DA TIMES 'N' STUFF ★

GUILTY

The trial of the century ended today with a guilty verdict by Judge Fudgie McGrudge.

Miami County resident Benjamin Krupp was sentenced to ten years at Piqua State Penitentiary for masterminding the robbery of Frank's Bank in Piqua nearly one year ago.

Two juveniles, George Beard and Harold Hutchins (both residents of Piqua), were also sentenced to ten years in the Piqua Juvenile Detention Center for their roles in the robbery.

Although all of the stolen money was recovered on the day of the robbery, Judge Fudgie McGrudge decided to make an example of the former elementary school principal and his two students by being a big meanie.

When asked to comment on the unusually harsh sentence, George Beard (age ten and three quarters) was reported to have said, "Aw, man!"

George's youthful accomplice, Harold Hutchins (age eleven) further expounded on the pair's reaction to the verdict by adding, "No fair!"

This guilty verdict ended the sensational scandal that stunned the world, received massive coverage in all of the news outlets, and interrupted the narrative flow of this book with a poorly drawn newspaper that contained a bunch of really tiny words.

Dr. Kent C. Toogood, president of Doctors United Movement to Banish Tiny Words in the Story (D.U.M.B. T.W.I.T.S.) warned that illustrations containing small words can cause eye strain, which could lead to headaches, nausea, and ridiculous acronyms.

Throughout the trial, many witnesses were called to testify against the defendants, including fellow classmate Melvin Sneedly. Melvin gave many long, soporifically detailed accounts of alleged irresponsible and disrespectful (to him) behavior by the two young defendants. He concluded his incendiary three-day testimonial by sticking out his tongue at Mr. Beard and Mr. Hutchins and singing the popular playground taunt, "Nyaa-Nyaa na Nyaa-Nyaa."

Other witnesses against the defendants included Piqua State Penitentiary inmate Dr. Diaper, former science teacher (and current resident of the Piqua Valley Home for the Reality-Challenged), Mr. Morty Fyde, and a small group of parents from Connecticut, North Dakota, California, Texas,

(continued on pages 2-49)

The cops slammed on the brakes, grabbed Mr. Krupp, handcuffed him, and threw him into the backseat of the car along with George and Harold.

Their trials lasted for nearly a year, and George, Harold, and Mr. Krupp were all found guilty. They were each sentenced to ten years of incarceration. This unusually harsh sentence was tough on George and Harold, but it was *REALLY* hard on Mr. Krupp!

CHAPTER 4
LIFE IN THE BIG HOUSE

Poor Mr. Krupp. He had been locked up at the
Piqua State Penitentiary for months, and the
life of a jailbird just wasn't his thing. All day
long he had people bossing him around. He ate
nutritionally deficient, horrible-tasting meals
in a filthy cafeteria. He got harassed constantly
by a bunch of meat-headed bullies, and he spent
his days doing menial "busy work" in an
overcrowded, poorly ventilated sweatshop.

Mr. Krupp was told when to eat, when to read, and when to exercise. He even had to ask permission to go to the bathroom! He was constantly bombarded with pointless rules, ridiculous discipline, random searches, metal detectors, security cameras, and pharmaceuticals designed to make everyone compliant and docile. It was a lot like being a student at Jerome Horwitz Elementary School, except that the prison had better funding.

Mr. Krupp grumbled angrily to himself as he stomped around the prison courtyard on a gloomy autumn afternoon. In the center of the courtyard, a giant green tarp shielded everyone's eyes from something large and tall that was being built in honor of the Piqua State Penitentiary's upcoming ten-year anniversary. Everyone assumed it was some kind of statue, but since nobody had seen this top-secret project (not even the warden), nobody was quite sure *what* it was.

"I'm sick of this place," Mr. Krupp muttered to himself. "Everybody's always telling me what to do! If *ONE MORE PERSON* gives me another order, I think I'm going to go *CRAZY*!"

"Hey, fatty!" shouted a tiny inmate working behind the green tarp. "Gimme that hammer over there!"

Mr. Krupp clenched his fists furiously. "YOU CAN'T TELL ME WHAT TO DO!" he screamed. "YOU'RE A PRISONER JUST LIKE I AM!"

"I most certainly am *nothing* like you," said the tiny prisoner. It was Tippy Tinkletrousers, who was serving an eight-year sentence for attempting to take over the planet with intent to enslave humanity.

Mr. Krupp rolled up his sweaty sleeves and stomped over to the pint-sized prisoner.

He eyed Tippy up and down. Tippy eyed Mr. Krupp down and up.

"Hey!" Mr. Krupp shouted. "You look kinda familiar!"

"I agree!" said Tippy. "But I can't quite remember where I've seen you before!"

The two men walked in slow circles around each other.

"Well, whoever you are," Mr. Krupp said, "you've got no business bossing me around!"

"I'll have you know," said Tippy, "that I'm MORE than just a regular prisoner! I'm an art-*eest*! I was *handpicked* to build a robo— er, I mean, a *statue* by Warden Schmorden."

Suddenly, a rotund little man peeped his bulbous, dandruff-speckled head out from behind the green tarp. "Did somebody just say my name?" he asked excitedly. It was Warden Gordon B. Schmorden, the guardian and chief jailer of Piqua State Penitentiary. Warden Schmorden was known far and wide for his cruelty and strictness. He once sentenced a prisoner to a year of solitary confinement just for ending a sentence with a preposition.

Warden Schmorden was undoubtedly the most maniacally evil person anyone had ever met, but the injurious jailer had one fatal weakness: He was easily flattered. And that weakness was exactly what Tippy Tinkletrousers used to talk his way into making a giant statue of Warden Gordon Bordon Schmorden, to commemorate the ten-year anniversary of the Piqua State Penitentiary.

"Just leave everything to me," said Tippy at the start of the project, "and I'll construct the most stunningly handsome statue you've ever seen!"

"Really?" said the warden. "can you make it extra tall and *extra* handsome?"

"Of course!" said Tippy.

"Wonderful, *WONDERFUL*!" cried Warden Schmorden. "How soon can you get started?"

"As soon as I get my supplies," said Tippy.

He handed the warden a carefully written list of tools and materials.

"Hey!" said Warden Schmorden, looking over the list. "Why do most of these supplies come from the Mad Scientist Mini-Mall? What do you need an *Emulsifying Sossilflange Inhibitor* for? And what kind of a statue uses a *Reverse-Somgobulating Tracto-McFractionalizer*?"

"You know," said Tippy, "I don't tell you how to run your prison — so don't tell me how to build my statues!"

"Fair enough!" said Warden Schmorden.

CHAPTER 5
THE UNVEILING

One brisk evening in late October, the entire prison was yawning with excitement. The prisoners had all gathered in the bleachers under a clear, moonlit sky, as the prison band played a slow, reverent, and deeply moving rendition of "Whoomp! (There It Is)." After everyone dried their eyes, Warden Gordon Bordon Schmorden stepped onto the stage to congratulate himself. He proudly bragged about his great humility, confessed his intense hatred of intolerant people, and spoke for hours about his legendary brevity.

Then the moment of truth arrived. Tippy Tinkletrousers's statue was finally ready to be shown to the world.

With great theatrical flair, Tippy proudly strutted out to the courtyard and grabbed hold of the giant green tarp.

"Gentlemen and gentlemen," he announced. "It gives me great pleasure to get the heck out of here!"

Tippy pulled on the tarp and revealed his creation.

"Hey!" shouted Warden Gordon Bordon
Schmorden. "That statue doesn't have a head!"

"It's not a statue!" yelled Tippy, as he
climbed a tall ladder up to the cockpit on
top. "It's a giant Robo-Suit! And after I escape
from this horrible prison, I'm going to put
an end to that nonsensical nuisance, Captain
Underpants!"

Tippy wiggled into the tiny cockpit and started up the engines. Suddenly, the colossal contraption came to life. Its mighty chest heaved as its gigantic, gorilla-like arms swayed threateningly.

"SOUND THE ALARMS!" screamed Warden Schmorden. "STOP THAT GUY!"

Armed guards ran in every direction while
sirens wailed and prisoners screamed for
their lives. Massive searchlights swept across
the sky as the metallic behemoth took its
first thunderous steps toward freedom.

Suddenly, Tippy stopped and thought for a moment. "Hey! I know where I saw that guy before!" he said. Tippy searched the crowds of panicking prisoners until he found the one he was looking for.

The giant hand of Tippy's Robo-Suit reached down and plucked Mr. Krupp from the crowd.

"I *KNEW* I'd recognized you from somewhere!" said Tippy. "You're the principal of that school I shrank last year!"

"Oh, yeeeaaaah!" said Mr. Krupp. "I remember you now! You're that *Professor Poopypants* guy."

"MY NAME IS *NOT* PROFESSOR POOPYPANTS!" screamed the angry villain. "*That* was a ridiculous name! So I changed it to Tippy Tinkletrousers!"

"Gee, that's a *lot* better!" said Mr. Krupp sarcastically.

Tippy glared into Mr. Krupp's defiant eyes. "I shall ignore your *impudence* on one condition!" Tippy said. "Tell me where I can find George Beard and Harold Hutchins!"

"George and Harold?" asked Mr. Krupp, as he dangled precariously from Tippy's giant robotic fingertips. "What do you want with those two?"

"Those boys have *something* to do with Captain Underpants!" said Tippy. "I've seen them all together. They know each other, *I'm sure of it*!"

"Well, they should be pretty easy to find!" said Mr. Krupp. "They're both locked up at the Piqua Juvenile Detention Center!"

"They're in *juvie*, eh?" said Tippy, with a sinister smirk. "Then that's where *we're* gonna go!"

Tippy clutched Mr. Krupp tightly in his robotic fist as he stomped forward, crushing the armored watchtower and smashing through Cell Block B.

"Freeze, or we'll shoot!" shouted the guards.

"How about if *I* shoot and *YOU* freeze?" said Tippy, as he pressed a button on his control panel, causing a giant door in the chest of his Robo-Suit to swing open. A massive laser shooter poked out from the mechanical depths of the Robo-Suit and zapped the armed guards. Suddenly, they were transformed into frozen statues.

47

"*WHAT DID YOU JUST DO?*" screamed Mr. Krupp hysterically.

"Oh, relax," said Tippy. "It's just my Freezy-Beam 4000. It temporarily freezes whatever it zaps, for as long as I choose. Those guards will thaw out in about ten minutes, and they'll be perfectly fine."

Tippy's heaving mechanical monstrosity thundered through the prison parking lot, battering buses and crushing cars as it headed toward the Piqua Juvenile Detention Center.

"I just don't get it," said Mr. Krupp. "What's so important about Captain Underpants?"

"That ridiculous superhero foiled my plot to take over the planet and enslave humanity!" shouted Tippy. "He's the reason I got locked up!"

"Everybody knows that," said Mr. Krupp, "but what's going to stop him from defeating you again?"

"Oh, don't you worry your sweaty little head about that," said Tippy. "I've got a few tricks up my sleeve *this time*!"

CHAPTER 6
CALLING CAPTAIN UNDERPANTS

Meanwhile, across town at the Piqua Juvenile Detention Center, George and Harold were getting ready for bed.

"You know," said George, "I don't really mind being stuck here in juvie."

"Yeah," said Harold. "It's not much different from our old school . . . except that they have library books here."

"And a music teacher," said George.

"And an art teacher," said Harold.

As the two boys discussed the similarities
between elementary school and forced
confinement in a harsh, authoritarian penal
institute, they heard the sounds of booming
footsteps getting louder and louder.

Soon, their entire building began to shake
violently with each thundering stride.

George and Harold dashed to their windows
and saw Tippy's terrifying Robo-Suit stomping
toward them, freezing anyone and everything
that stood in its way.

"Oh, NO!" screamed Harold. "We're DOOMED!"

Tippy stopped at the main entrance to the
center and demanded to speak with whoever
was in charge. After a few minutes, the center's
administrator, Director Hector Schmector,
showed up nervously at the door.

"Umm . . ." said Director Schmector.
"M-M-May I help you?"

"Do you have two kids in there named
George Beard and Harold Hutchins?"
shouted Tippy.

"Uh, yeah," said Director Schmector.
"Those two kids are nothing but trouble.
They're always pulling pranks, too! I mean,
you can't sit on a toilet around here without
getting ketchup sprayed in your underwear!
And last week, they—"

"*JUST HAND THEM OVER!*" Tippy
interrupted.

"Hey, no *prob*!" Director Schmector
chuckled, trying to sound cool.

Director Hector Schmector pranced excitedly to George and Harold's cell, grabbed them by the arms, and escorted them to the front door. "This'll teach you for putting hair remover in my shampoo!" said Director Schmector.

Hector tossed the boys outside and locked the door. George and Harold stood trembling before Tippy's massive Robo-Suit as the crazed inventor chuckled menacingly.

"Hello, George and Harold!" crowed Tippy. "Remember me?"

The boys were too frightened to speak.

"Hey, Tippy," said Mr. Krupp. "You don't need me anymore, do you? I mean, I told you where you could find the brats, right? You can let me go now, right?"

"I guess so," said Tippy. He set Mr. Krupp down on the ground by George and Harold.

"Ha!" Mr. Krupp laughed. "I never thought I'd be happy to see *you two kids* again! You bubs are in BIG TROUBLE NOW!"

Almost without thinking, George and Harold reached out their hands and snapped their fingers.

SNAP!
SNAP!

Suddenly, a ridiculously optimistic smile spread across Mr. Krupp's face.

"Hey!" cried Tippy. "What's going on down there?"

What George and Harold knew, and what Tippy was about to discover, was that Mr. Krupp was transforming into the world's greatest superhero: Captain Underpants.

Quickly, he wiggled out of his purple prison jumpsuit, flipped his shoes away, and peeled off his sweaty toupee. The only thing missing was his cape. He looked around the detention center but couldn't find anything suitable. "I can't be a superhero without a cape," said Captain Underpants.

"You're OK!" George assured him.

"Yeah!" said Harold. "You don't need a cape! Seriously!"

"Sorry," said the Captain, "but ya *gotta* look fine if you're gonna fight crime!"

And with no time to spare, Captain Underpants flew off to find a cape.

"That—*that guy was Captain Underpants*?!!?" cried Tippy.

"*Doyee!*" said George.

"AAAUGH!" screamed Tippy. "I JUST HAD HIM IN MY HAND!!! I COULD HAVE CRUSHED HIM!!!"

Again, George responded with the only intelligent word that could possibly be applied in such a situation: *"Doyee!"*

Meanwhile, Captain Underpants had flown
to a nearby shopping center, which was
having its Semiannual Lazy Storytelling Sale.

"Quick!" cried Captain Underpants. "Do
you guys sell superhero capes?"

"You betcha!" said the employee cheerfully.
"They're in aisle thirty-nine between the
diaries and the wizard hats!"

"Awesome!" cried Captain Underpants.

In no time at all, our hero found a cape,
tied it around his neck, and flew off into the
night to face his mortal enemy.

CHAPTER 7
TIPPY'S TROUSER TROUBLES

Meanwhile, back at the Piqua Juvenile Detention Center, Tippy Tinkletrousers was in a tizzy! He grabbed George and Harold in his mighty robotic hands and demanded some answers.

"Tell me everything you know about Captain Underpants," screamed Tippy, "or I'll squish you kids like a couple of blueberries!"

"Well," said George, "he's really strong!"

"And," said Harold, "he's really powerful!"

"Yes, yes," said Tippy. "What *else* is he?"

"*He's right behind you!*" said George and
Harold simultaneously.

Tippy turned quickly, but not quickly
enough. Captain Underpants swung his flabby
fist and bashed Tippy right in the jaw.

The force of the blow sent Tippy's Robo-Suit flying over the top of the Juvenile Detention Center and into one of Piqua's many downtown skyscrapers.

George and Harold flew from the grip of Tippy's Robo-Fists and landed safely in some nearby bushes.

"I'll keeeeel YOU!" screamed Tippy, as
he pulled himself up and lunged at Captain
Underpants. The chest panel of the Robo-Suit
flipped open and a brilliant burst of energy
from the Freezy-Beam 4000 shot out at the
Waistband Warrior. But Captain Underpants
was too quick. He zipped and zinged, expertly
avoiding every frozen energy beam that burst
from the belly of the beastly Robo-Suit.

ZING!

"Oh, *Tippy*!" called Captain Underpants, as he sat coyly atop a nearby skyscraper. "I'm up here!"

Tippy turned quickly and zapped his Freezy-Beam 4000 at the skyscraper, covering it with a thick casing of ice. But Captain Underpants had been too fast. He had zinged away just in time.

Captain Underpants flew several blocks away, to the swing set at the playground of Jerome Horwitz Elementary School. Robo-Tippy ran after him.

"Yoo-hoo! *Tippy-Tip!*" Captain Underpants sang, as he swung playfully from a swing. "Will you give me a push?"

Tippy leaped over the school and landed in the football field.

He zapped his Freezy-Beam 4000 again,
this time covering the swing set with a thick
coating of ice. But again, Captain Underpants
had zanged away just in time.

"Heeeere, Tippy, Tippy, Tippy!" called
Captain Underpants again, as he lounged lazily
between Tippy's giant robotic feet. "I'm down
here now! Could I have some ice, please?"

"Why you little—" screamed Tippy, as he
bent over and zapped his Freezy-Beam 4000
down between his feet.

Of course, Captain Underpants was long
gone before the ice beam reached the ground.
Unfortunately for Tippy, however, his Robo-
Feet weren't.

Tippy's giant Robo-Feet and Robo-Legs
were now encased in a huge, shimmering
iceberg. He pulled with all his might, but his
whole lower half was frozen to the football
field. Tippy was stuck.

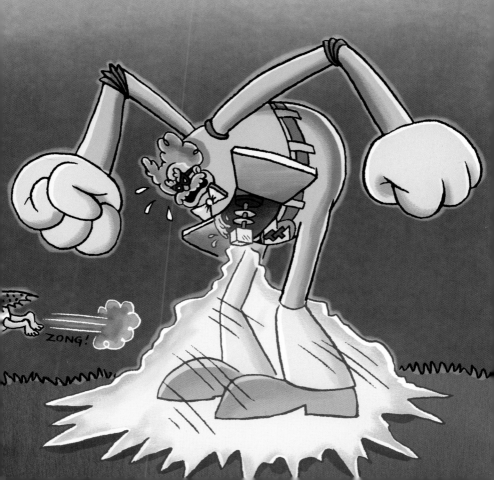

ZONG!

CHAPTER 8
BREAK IN TWO:
ELECTRIC BOOGALOO

"NOOOOOO!" screamed Tippy. He ducked his head beneath the cockpit of the Robo-Suit and disappeared down a stairwell into the intricate innards of his intimidating invention.

Captain Underpants grabbed the arms of the Robo-Suit and began to pull. Harder and harder he tugged until, one by one, the rivets in the Robo-Suit's thick steel belt began to pop. The harder Captain Underpants yanked, the more the Robo-Suit began to break in two.

The shrieking sounds of twisting metal reverberated around Tippy as he traversed the crumbling staircase. His only chance was to make it down to the lower half of the Robo-Suit before Captain Underpants pulled it apart.

With no time to spare, Tippy dashed into
the Robo-Pants, just as the Robo-Suit broke
in two.

"You haven't seen the last of me!" Tippy yelled, as he closed the emergency hatch on the Robo-Pants. Then, Tippy set his Tinkle-Time Travelometer to "Five Years Ago" and pressed the "Away We Go!" button.

Suddenly, sparks of blue lightning began emanating from the Robo-Pants. The massive bolts crackled loudly and grew more and more intense until finally, Tippy and his Robo-Pants were enveloped in a giant ball of blue lightning.

A blinding flash turned the night sky into day for a sliver of a second, and then it was all over. Tippy and his Robo-Pants had disappeared, leaving only an empty mound of ice behind. The crazed inventor and his terrifying trousers would never be seen again after that night. They would, however, be seen exactly five years *before* that night . . .

But before I can tell you that story, we have to go back *even further* . . .

CHAPTER 9
EXACTLY FIVE YEARS, ELEVEN DAYS, FOURTEEN HOURS, AND SIX MINUTES AGO . . .

This is Harold Hutchins.

Harold is six years old, and he lives with his mom and sister at 1520 Vine Street in Piqua, Ohio.

Harold's parents had just gotten divorced, and his dad had moved to Nevada about six months ago. None of this had been easy for Harold. He didn't talk about it. In fact, Harold Hutchins didn't talk much at all. He kept to himself, mostly, and drew pictures. Lots and lots of pictures.

Harold liked to draw monsters and superheroes. The monsters he created were evil and ferocious, and his superheroes were always virtuous and brave. They were never far away when you needed them.

Harold loved getting lost in his wonderful paper-and-pencil adventures, where the good guys always won and the bad guys always ended up getting the "kick in the pants" that they deserved.

Today had started out just like any ordinary school day. Harold got dressed and ate his breakfast, trying hard not to think about the tough day that lay ahead of him. Harold was in kindergarten at Jerome Horwitz Elementary School, and he hated every minute of it. His teacher was mean, the bullies were jerks, and the principal was just plain *evil*. The best Harold could do was try to "fit in" and not draw any unnecessary attention to himself. He brushed his teeth and carefully placed his pencils and his favorite drawings into his backpack, unaware that today was going to be a day that would change his life forever.

Harold's mom helped him put his backpack on at the front door.

"Maybe you'll make a friend at school today," she said cheerfully.

"Nah," said Harold, emotionless. "I don't think so."

"What about that little boy next door who moved in last weekend?" said Harold's mom. "What's his name?"

Harold shrugged. He had seen the boy once or twice, but they hadn't actually met.

"Maybe you should go over and introduce yourself," said Harold's mom. "Wouldn't it be nice to have a friend who lives next door?"

Harold shrugged again.

Harold's mom hugged him and kissed the top of his head. She got two dollars out of her purse and handed them to Harold. "This is for your lunch, OK, honey?" she said. "I don't want you using this money at the candy machine or the pop machine!"

"I won't," said Harold.

That much was true. Harold knew his lunch money would never make it to the candy machine or the pop machine. Harold's two dollars usually never even made it into the school. They were always taken away from him by a sixth-grade bully named Kipper.

Kipper Krupp was the biggest and meanest kid at Jerome Horwitz Elementary School. He was the captain of the wrestling team *AND* the nephew of the school principal, so everybody treated him like *royalty*.

Kipper's three creepy friends, Loogie, Bugg, and Finkstein, also got special treatment, and they all paraded up and down the school hallways like they owned the place.

Every day, Kipper and his three friends stole lunch money from the kindergartners. Most of the kids just handed it over without question. It was a lot less trouble (and much less painful) than getting a wedgie or a punch in the stomach. Kipper Krupp loved to terrorize kindergartners, and there was nothing anybody could do about it. If Kipper ever got into a jam, all he had to do was call on his uncle, Principal Krupp.

"Uncle Benny!" Kipper would cry. "That kindergartner just hit my fist with her stomach!"

"Oh, she *DID*, did she?" Mr. Krupp would yell, turning to the small child writhing in pain on the floor. "How DARE you hurt my nephew's fist?!!?" Mr. Krupp had a ZERO-TOLERANCE policy in place at Jerome Horwitz Elementary School, and he was very strict about it. He had once suspended a third grader just for saying the word "gun." To be honest, the boy had actually said the word "gum," but it *sounded* a lot like "gun," and there was no room for common sense when it came to ZERO TOLERANCE.

79

Harold knew from experience that the
wisest thing to do was stay out of Kipper's way,
so his daily walk to school became more like
an obstacle course. He quickly ran in spurts,
dashing from trash can to mailbox to tree,
hiding behind anything he could find, just in
case Kipper and his friends were nearby.

The worst section of Harold's mad dash to
school was the intersection of Dogwood Drive
and Rosita Lane. There was nowhere to hide
between the big tree by the coffee shop and
the sign at the gas station across the street. He
just had to wait for the walk signal, run for it,
and hope for the best. Most days, Harold was
lucky. But his luck was about to run out.

Harold crouched quietly behind the coffee shop tree, watching the traffic lights, concentrating on the cars, and looking out for Kipper. It was very stressful. After a couple of minutes, the cars came to a stop, the walk signal lit up, and Harold took one last glance left and right. It was now or never. He jumped up and ran across the street as fast as he could go. When he reached the other side of the street, Harold leaped behind the display sign in front of the gas station. He had made it! He was safe . . . *or so he thought.*

"HEY, YOU STUPID KID!" shouted Billy Bill, the owner of the gas station. "GIT AWAY FROM THAT SIGN!" Harold's heart was pounding in his throat as Billy Bill stomped toward him and grabbed the back of his T-shirt. He yanked Harold out from behind the sign, making a terrible scene. "THAT SIGN IS A VALUABLE PIECE OF MERCHANDISE," Billy Bill screamed, "NOT A *TOY* FOR YOU TO PLAY WITH!"

"I'm sorry, I'm sorry!" Harold whispered, frantically trying to pull away. But it was too late. Billy Bill's loud shouting had caught the attention of Kipper Krupp and his three creepy companions. The four bullies strutted across the street toward Harold.

"Hey, kid!" yelled Kipper. "Why are you bothering this nice man?"

"I'm sorry!" Harold said again, looking down. Billy Bill released Harold with a shove, causing him to fall to the ground.

"You boys better take care of your little friend there," Billy Bill said, "or I'm gonna call the cops on him!"

"Don't worry, Mister," said Kipper with an evil grin. "We'll take *good* care of him!"

Kipper yanked Harold up by his arm while Loogie pulled Harold's backpack open and started rummaging through it. "Hey, look! I found his lunch money," said Loogie.

"Gimme it!" yelled Kipper. Loogie dutifully put the money into Kipper's moist, dirty hand.

None of this behavior appeared to disturb Billy Bill at all. In fact, he seemed to enjoy watching it.

"You gotta learn to stick up for yourself, boy," Billy Bill said to Harold, chuckling, "or people are gonna bully you your whole life!"

The four fiends dragged Harold across the street, toward the school parking lot. Harold's luck was running out. But fortunately, as we all know, luck has a way of changing. And Harold's bad luck was about to change in a very BIG way.

CHAPTER 10
MEET GEORGE

This is George Beard.

George is five-and-three-quarters years old. He and his parents had just moved from Michigan into the house next door to Harold and his family. George was what adults like to call a "precocious" child. His mother had taught him to read and write when he was four years old, and he currently scored higher on tests than most children twice his age.

George's former teachers had suggested that he skip ahead to the third grade, but his parents decided it would be better if George stayed in a classroom with kids his own age. To this day, George's parents were still not sure if they had made the right decision. On the one hand, George had developed good social skills and had been well liked by his classmates. That was good. On the other hand, George was bored in class and often got into mischief. That was bad.

George had never really liked school very much. He preferred riding his skateboard, watching monster movies, and reading comics and graphic novels. George liked writing stories, too. He had filled up more than twenty spiral notebooks with marvelously silly adventure stories that he had written all by himself.

Many of George's stories had gotten him into trouble when he read them out loud at his old school. His classmates loved them, but his teachers thought they were rude, violent, and totally inappropriate.

"I hope things will be better here in Ohio," said George's mother, as she helped him get ready for his very first day of classes at Jerome Horwitz Elementary School. "Your father and I bought you this nice tie to wear at school today."

"A *TIE*?" cried George. "Kids don't wear ties!"

"Well, *you're* going to wear one," said George's mother. "I want you to make a good *first impression*!"

"Aw, come on, Mom!" said George. "Ties are for nerds!"

"Oh, for heaven's sake!" said George's mom. "Your father wears a tie. Is he a nerd?"

"Umm . . . *kind of*," said George.

"Don't be ridiculous!" said George's mom. "You're wearing a tie, and that's *FINAL*!"

"Rats!" said George.

George put his backpack on and reluctantly hugged his mom at the door. (He was still a little upset about the whole "tie" thing.)

"Have a good first day at school, dear," said George's mom.

"Mm-hmmm," said George.

George grabbed his skateboard from the bushes by the driveway and started off toward school. It was about five blocks away, and the sidewalks were mostly smooth with hardly any pebbles. Good for skateboarding.

The ride to school had been very pleasant, actually, until George reached the corner of Dogwood Drive and Rosita Lane. There was some kind of commotion going on in front of the gas station across the street, and George watched it intently as he waited for the traffic light to change. He saw the gas station guy shove a yellow-haired kid to the ground. Then he saw some mean-looking kids yank the boy up and steal his money. This was not good.

Finally, the light changed, and George walked across the street toward the gas station. He stood by the display sign while the attendant laughed at the yellow-haired kid and told him he needed to learn to stick up for himself. George was furious.

CHAPTER 11
FURIOUS GEORGE

There is not a whole lot you can do when you are a little kid who encounters injustice. Your natural desire is to set things right, but that can often backfire, resulting in even *greater* injustices. The sad truth is, big people usually have all of the power. You can't force anybody to be kind or fair or honorable, especially if you're only forty-three inches tall and weigh only fifty pounds.

That's why it's important to be smart.

FREE BRAKE INSPECTION

George Beard had just witnessed the most
hostile and unfair thing he had ever seen.
The bad guys outnumbered him by five to
one and outweighed him by probably 700
pounds. But George was smarter than all of
them put together, and he knew it.

As the bullies dragged Harold across the
street, George looked around him for the
best way to make things right. He focused
in on the display sign next to him. The sign
read FREE BRAKE INSPECTION. This was a
busy intersection, and George knew that a
tiny change on this sign could create a great
deal of pandemonium, so he reached over
to the sign and removed the letters *k* and *e*
from the word *brake*.

"*HEY!*" screamed Billy Bill. "YOU GIT
AWAY FROM THAT SIGN RIGHT NOW,
Y'HEAR?!!? WHAT IS *WRONG* WITH YOU
KIDS THESE DAYS?!!?"

Billy Bill marched over to George, yelling
and waving his hands in the air frantically.
He reached out to grab George by the shirt
collar, but he never got the chance.

At that very moment, a violet Volkswagen jumped the curb and screeched up next to Billy Bill. Two old ladies flew out of the car, screaming at the top of their lungs!

"Free *BRA* inspection?!!?" shouted the driver, as she smacked Billy Bill over the head with her purse. "That's *OFFENSIVE*!!!"

"HOW *DARE* YOU?!!?" yelled the other lady, hitting Billy Bill with her cane. "Women are human beings, not *toys* for you to play with!"

"You're a MALE CHAUVINIST PIG!"
screamed a third lady, who had run over
from the coffee shop across the street with a
group of her angry female friends. They each
took turns kicking Billy Bill repeatedly in the
knees, as other women drivers slammed on
their brakes and rushed forward to join in
the ferocious female fight for equality.

"You gotta learn to stick up for yourself,"

George said to Billy Bill,
smiling, "or people are gonna
bully you your whole life!"

George walked past the giant traffic jam
that was forming and ignored Billy Bill's
tear-filled cries for mercy as the kicking and
whacking and hair-pulling and foot-stomping
continued. George was looking for that
yellow-haired kid.

He skateboarded over to the elementary school and circled back toward the parking lot. There he saw Kipper and his creepy cohorts laughing and cheering as they tore up Harold's drawings and snapped each of his pencils in half.

"LEAVE HIM ALONE!" shouted George.

The sixth-grade bullies turned and looked at the tiny kindergartner who stood defiantly before them.

"Haw! Haw! Haw!" laughed Kipper. "Whatcha gonna do if we don't?"

"I'm gonna *Indiana Jones* ya!" George said, as he untied his tie and twirled it threateningly between his outstretched hands.

"GET HIM!" yelled Kipper. The bullies ran in for the attack, and George let them have it.

CHAPTER 12
THE INCREDIBLY GRAPHIC VIOLENCE CHAPTER (IN FLIP-O-RAMA™)

PILKEY® BRAND

⊃-RAMA

HERE'S HOW IT WORKS!

STEP 1
First, place your *left* hand inside the dotted lines marked "LEFT HAND HERE." Hold the book open *flat*.

STEP 2
Grasp the *right-hand* page with your right thumb and index finger (inside the dotted lines marked "RIGHT THUMB HERE").

STEP 3
Now *quickly* flip the right-hand page back and forth until the picture appears to be *animated*.

(For extra fun, try adding your own sound-effects!)

FLIP-O-RAMA

(pages 103 and 105)

Remember, flip *only* page 103.
While you are flipping, be sure you
can see the picture on page 103
and the one on page 105.
If you flip quickly, the two
pictures will start to look like
<u>one</u> *animated* picture.

Don't forget to
add your own sound-effects!

LEFT HAND HERE

THE KIPPER
WHIPPER

RIGHT
THUMB
HERE

RIGHT
INDEX
FINGER
HERE

104

THE KIPPER
WHIPPER

Kipper screamed like a giant
blubbering baby and ran for his life.
Bugg and Loogie were up next.

LEFT HAND HERE

THE ATTACKER
SMACKER

107

RIGHT
THUMB
HERE

RIGHT
INDEX
FINGER
HERE

108

THE ATTACKER
SMACKER

"Let's get out of here!" screamed Loogie
and Bugg through their tears.
Finkstein opened up a trash bin and
the four bullies tried to scramble inside.
But they weren't fast enough!

LEFT HAND HERE

THE TORMENTER
PREVENTER

111

RIGHT
THUMB
HERE

RIGHT
INDEX
FINGER
HERE

112

THE TORMENTER
PREVENTER

CHAPTER 13
THE DETENTION

"I don't want you guys messing with me ever again!" George said firmly, as the bullies squealed in high-pitched terror. "And that yellow-haired kid is off-limits, too! You mess with us, you answer to *The TIE*!"

George snapped his tie in the air one last time, causing the four sobbing sixth graders to shriek like baboons.

"Uh-Uh-Uncle BENNY!" Kipper wailed through his tears.

Suddenly, Mr. Krupp came storming out of the building. *"WHAT'S GOING ON OUT HERE?"* he screamed.

"That little kid beat us up!" Kipper sobbed.

"Oh, he *DID*, did he?" yelled Mr. Krupp, as he grabbed George by his arm. "I don't take kindly to *bullies* in this school!"

"They're the bullies!" cried Harold, pointing at Kipper and his three frightened friends. "Those guys were just about to beat that kid up . . . He was just defending himself!"

Mr. Krupp reached over and grabbed Harold by his arm. "I don't like *LIARS,* either!" he growled.

Mr. Krupp yanked both boys to the detention room. "You two troublemakers are going to stay here until you've learned your lesson!" he shouted, then slammed the door.

"So much for a good first impression," said George.

The two boys sat in silence for several minutes. Harold opened his backpack and took out a notebook and the pointy half of one of his broken pencils. He started to draw.

"What grade are you in?" asked George.

"Kindergarten," said Harold.

"Me, too," said George. "I'm new. We just moved here three days ago."

"Oh," said Harold. "I think you live next door to my house."

"Really?" said George.

George glanced over and noticed that Harold was drawing a giant monster.

"Hey, you're a good drawer," George said.

"Thanks," said Harold.

George watched as Harold drew a flying hero zapping the monster with a laser beam.

"Cool!" said George, pointing to the superhero. "What's that guy's name?"

Harold shrugged. "He doesn't have a name."

"How come?" asked George.

Harold shrugged again. "It's just a picture," he said. "It's not really a story."

"Oh," said George.

George watched intently as Harold finished his picture. When he was done, Harold folded the page back and started drawing a new picture on the next page.

"Um . . . do you want to draw, too?" Harold asked. "I have some more pencils. They're broken, but the pointy parts still work OK."

"No," said George. "I can't draw good. I'm a writer."

"Oh," said Harold. He tore some fresh pages out from the back of his notebook and handed them to George. "Here. You can write on these if you want."

George took the papers and thought for a long time. Then he wrote *The Adventures of Dog Man* at the top of the first page. At the bottom he wrote *By George and . . .*

"Hey, what's your name, kid?" George asked.

"Harold," said Harold.

George wrote Harold's name down at the bottom. "I'm gonna write a comic book," said George. "You can draw the pictures, OK?"

"Umm . . . OK," said Harold.

And that is how George and Harold
became friends and started their publishing
empire on the very same day.

the ADVENCHERS OF DOG MAN

AKShin

LaFFs

FLeas

By George and Harold

The adVenchers of
DOG MAN
by George and Harold
One Time there was a POLISE guy.
His partnor was a DOG named GreG
they were GOOD at caching crimenals and STUFF
OW
But one Day there was a Bom.
We haf to stop the Bom Greg
Bom

But they were too Late
KaBLEWY
the Bom Blew up and they Got Hurt-ed.
a ambyewLense tooked them to the HospitteL
How Do you FeeL old Fre-nd?.
RUFF
Me Too

And SO

HORAY FOR DOGMAN!

DOGman was the Best of all cops.

He cood sniff crooks with his DOG nose.

rats

SNIFF SNIFF

He cood Hear crimes with his DOG ears.

rats

and Best of all he cood Punch Crimenels with his humen fists

OW

POW

I mean Bats!

QUICK DOG man. where is the crook?

ROOF ROOF

Hes up on the roof!

What IS He wearing?

Pant Pant Pant Pant

Hes wearing Pants!

DoG Man Was the Gratest cop of ever!

But He had one mortel Fear...

vack ume cleenor

DoG Man saw the vackume cleenor. He runned and hided.

OH I FORGOT. Dogs Are ascared of vackume cleenors!!!

DOG man RUNNed to save the day

BUT then...

VRRR

DOG man RUNNed away

ILL get YOU DOG man

HE RUNNed and RUNNed

Finely DOG man GOT cornered in a corner.

I'll Keel yeew!

the vackume cleenor got closer and closerer.

DoG man Got scarder and scarderer.

The vackume ROBOT Leeped attackishly

But then LOOKiT what happend.

POP

The vackume got unpluged

DOG man wasint ascared no more!

He Beated up the ROBOT

POW

Then He FOLLOWED the cord

it Leaded strate to Peteys Hideout

secrit Hideout

UH OH

then Petey Got arestid

rats if only I wood of made that cord six inches Longer.

DOG man Was the hero

CHAPTER 15
THE PLAN

Mr. Krupp's day had been very busy, and he'd completely forgotten all about the two boys he had banished to the detention room. By the time the final bell rang at 2:45, George and Harold had finished their very first comic book.

"Hey, this comic book turned out pretty good," said George.

"Yep," said Harold, smiling.

"I bet we could make copies of this and sell them for twenty-five cents each!" said George.

The two boys gathered their things and walked out the front door of the school.

"We should start our own comic book company," said Harold.

"Let's do it!" said George. "We can call it Tree House Comix, Inc.!"

"Why *Tree House*?" asked Harold.

"Cuz my dad is building me a tree house in our backyard!" said George. "It's going to have electricity and a TV and everything! We can make our comic books up there!"

"Awesome!" said Harold.

George and Harold walked by the trash bin where Kipper and his friends were just about to administer *killer wedgies* to a couple of kindergartners.

"Oh, *Kippy*," called George.

The bullies turned and saw George reaching for his tie. Suddenly, their eyes filled with horror. They released their prey and ran away, waving their arms and yipping like wiener dogs.

"I think I'm going to wear a tie every day from now on!" said George.

"I think that's a good idea," said Harold.

As George and Harold walked home, the two friends talked about their favorite movies and games, which videos were the funniest, and what kind of bubble gum blew the best bubbles.

"Mmmm," said Harold. "All that talk about bubble gum is making me hungry!"

"C'mon over to my house," said George. "I make a *mean* peanut-butter-and-gummy-worm sandwich!"

"Really?" said Harold.

"Yep!" George said. "The secret is the chocolate syrup!"

"OK," said Harold.

Soon the boys reached George's house and headed for the backyard. George's dad was hard at work building George's new tree house.

"Hi, Pop!" said George.

"Hey, buddy," said George's dad, "how was your first day at your new school?"

"OK," said George.

"And who's your new friend?" George's dad asked.

"This is Harold," said George. "He's a good drawer."

"Hello, Harold," said George's dad.

"Hi," said Harold.

"Well, we've got a lot of work to do, Pop," said George. "Do you want us to bring you a peanut-butter-and-gummy-worm sandwich?"

"Er—no, thank you," said George's dad.

The two new friends walked into George's house, made some sandwiches, and got right to work. George and Harold knew it was up to them to put a stop to Kipper Krupp's reign of terror. So they made a long list of Kipper's strengths and weaknesses to get a better understanding of their mortal enemy.

After a few minutes, Harold began to feel discouraged.

"This is terrible," said Harold. "Kipper Krupp has so many *strengths*! I can only think of one weakness!"

"What's that?" asked George.

"Well, he's kinda dumb," said Harold.

George smiled and wrote down *kinda dumb* under *weaknesses*. "That's all we need," said George.

CHAPTER 16
SUPER SPIES

The next day at school, Harold stuck close to George. The two boys spent their every free moment spying on Kipper and gathering as much information as they could about their enemy.

They wrote down Kipper's locker number and the type of padlock he used. They took note of Kipper's schedule and paid special attention to what he normally did between classes. They took measurements and even stayed after school to spy on Kipper's wrestling practices. By the end of the week, George and Harold knew Kipper's schedule better than Kipper knew it.

Kipper Krupp was a creature of habit. Every day, he did the exact same things at the exact same times. At the end of every school day, Kipper would go to his locker and unlock his heavy-duty padlock with a key he kept on a thick metal chain around his neck. Kipper would place his padlock on top of his locker, then open the locker door. Next, Kipper would empty his pockets, putting his valuables inside the locker. His phone always went on the top shelf, and the money he'd stolen from the kindergartners would always get crammed into a duffel bag at the bottom of the locker. Finally, Kipper would grab his padlock from the top of the locker, put it back on the door, and click it shut to lock it.

After wrestling practice, Kipper would
go back to his locker and unlock it the very
same way. He'd retrieve his phone, grab
his heavy-duty padlock from the top of his
locker, and put it back on the door. Finally,
he'd click it shut to lock everything back up
again. Surprisingly, Kipper usually left all of
his stolen money in his locker every night.
Perhaps Kipper thought the money was
safest in his locker. Nobody could open that
locker without a key, nobody but Kipper had
the key, and Kipper *never* took the key off
of his neck . . . not even in the *shower*!

"We'll never get that key away from Kipper," said Harold, as the two boys walked up the aisles of the local hardware store.

"We don't need the key," said George. "We just need this!" George picked up a brand-new padlock from the home security section. "This is the exact same kind of padlock that Kipper uses on his locker," said George.

"But it won't have the same key," said Harold. "Each one has a different key!"

"I know," said George.

"So how is *that* padlock going to help us?" asked Harold.

"You'll see . . ." said George, smiling.

After the boys paid for their brand-new heavy-duty padlock, they went to the toy shop across the street.

Down at the end of aisle three, near the beads and jewelry, George found what he was looking for: a Susie Sunshine Friendship Bracelet Kit.

"What is *THAT* for?" asked Harold.

"We've gotta make a couple of friendship bracelets this weekend," said George.

"Why? What for?" said Harold.

"You'll see . . ." said George, smiling even more.

That weekend, George and Harold spent a lot of time drawing up plans and designing pranks that would help put an end to the bully situation at Jerome Horwitz Elementary School. Then the two boys went through their homes, collecting everything they needed for the job. George found a long roll of shelf-lining paper in his kitchen and measured it carefully.

"Hey, Mom, can we have this?" said George. "It's for school."

"I suppose so," said George's mom.

Harold found some old pants and dress shoes that his dad had left behind when he moved away. He was pretty sure his dad wouldn't mind if they nailed them to George's wooden stilts.

"I still don't understand how we're going to hide these stilts in the school," said George, as he practiced walking on them.

"You'll see . . ." said Harold, who knew a few tricks of his own.

CHAPTER 17
MONDAY

On Monday morning, the boys woke up early,
gathered their supplies, and headed to school
about fifteen minutes before the rest of the
students started to arrive. George and Harold
carried their stilts and supplies into the boys'
restroom upstairs and placed them inside
one of the empty stalls.

Finally, they closed the stall door and locked it.

If you were standing outside the stall, looking underneath the door, it appeared as if somebody was sitting down in there *taking care of business*. George and Harold knew that nobody would dare go near this stall, so it was now the safest place in the school to hide stuff.

Soon the students began arriving and the day started pretty much like normal. Mr. Krupp marched up and down the hallways screaming and making children cry, Kipper and his creeps stole money and distributed wedgies to the kindergartners, and a general feeling of hopelessness and despair filled the morning air.

At lunchtime, as usual, the downtrodden kindergartners sat at their table with no food at all. Mr. Krupp stomped up to the kindergarten table and started getting angry. "How come you kids never have any food at lunchtime?" he shouted.

"Um . . ." said one kid, "we're on diets."

"Oh," said Mr. Krupp, as he pulled his belt up over his giant stomach. "Well, good!" he said. "It's important to stay fit and healthy like me!"

In the afternoon, George and Harold asked
to be excused so they could use the restroom.
They only had about five minutes to set things
up, so they had to hurry. Harold opened the
locked door of their secret restroom stall, and
George climbed up on the stilts. Quickly, they
sneaked out into the hallway.

George stilt-walked over to Kipper's locker, and Harold handed him the long spool of shelf-lining paper. Carefully, George placed the paper on top of the lockers and rolled it down to the end. The paper flipped over the edge of the locker tops and rolled down the side. Harold caught it and taped it to the side of the lockers, marking off some measurements with a ruler.

George put the padlock that he and Harold had bought on the end of the paper, two lockers down from Kipper's. They were ready. Quickly, they put their supplies back into the restroom stall, locked the door, and hurried back to their classroom.

At the end of the day, Kipper walked to his locker as usual. He unlocked his lock with the key hanging around his neck, then put his padlock on top of his locker (right on top of the long roll of paper). George and Harold were standing about six lockers away, where Harold had taped the end of the paper to the side of the long row of lockers. Now came the tricky part.

As Harold provided "cover," George carefully
pulled at the long roll of paper. The paper
began to move. Kipper's padlock, which was
just above Kipper's head, began to move away
from Kipper. George and Harold's padlock,
which was two lockers away, began moving
toward Kipper. Harold had measured
everything carefully, so George knew to
pull the paper exactly twenty-four inches.

When he was finished pulling, the new padlock was directly above Kipper's locker.

Kipper had just finished stuffing all of his stolen money into his duffel bag. He put his phone on the top shelf of his locker, closed the door, then reached up and grabbed George and Harold's padlock. Next he closed the door and clicked the new padlock on securely.

"Let's boogie!" said Kipper to his buddies, and they strutted to the gymnasium to get ready for wrestling practice.

"That was *AWESOME*!" said Harold.

"Yeah," said George. "But we've still got a lot of work to do!"

George and Harold waited patiently until almost everybody had gone home. Some kids were still in the gym, or outside, or in the chess club downstairs, but the hallways and restrooms were empty.

George and Harold sneaked over to Kipper's locker, unlocked their padlock, and opened the door.

Harold unzipped Kipper's duffel bag and emptied all of the stolen money onto the floor.

"Whoa!" said Harold. "There must be a thousand dollars here!" Harold quickly scooped up the stolen cash while George typed on Kipper's phone.

"What are you doing with that phone?" asked Harold.

"I'm sending a text to Kipper's three goons!" said George.

Once the money was safe and the texts were sent, George and Harold put everything back the way it was . . . *with two additions*. Harold put the Susie Sunshine Friendship Bracelet Kit in Kipper's locker, and George placed an envelope beside Kipper's phone.

Finally, George grabbed Kipper's padlock from the top of the lockers, closed the door, and locked it with Kipper's own padlock. Then they set everything up so it would be ready for tomorrow afternoon.

"Let's get out of here," Harold said nervously.

"Just one more thing," said George.

Quickly, the boys sneaked into the gym locker room and left a second envelope inside one of Kipper's smelly shoes. Then they hurried out of the school and headed for home.

"I kinda wish we could stay and watch the fireworks," said Harold.

"I think it's better if we're not there," said George. "Things are about to get ugly!"

CHAPTER 18

THINGS GET UGLY

Kipper found the envelope in his shoe just after wrestling practice ended. He opened it. Inside were two friendship bracelets and a note addressed to him. Kipper proudly slipped each friendship bracelet onto his wrist and admired them. He couldn't wait to show his buddies . . .

. . . who were all out in the hallway staring at their phones in shock.

"Look what I got!" Kipper said, proudly waving his wrist at his goons.

Kipper's friends, who were all reading the same text on their phones, looked up at Kipper with their mouths hanging open in disbelief.

"*What?*" said Kipper. "They're just friendship bracelets!"

Text message

From: Kipper Krupp

Lets make frendship braselits! Get ur supplise @ my Locker! Whoevr makes the prittyest one gets a big kiss from ME !!!!!

Options   Back

Kipper's three friends looked at each other like Kipper had gone completely mad.

"I don't want to make friendship bracelets with you, dude," said Loogie.

"Me neither," said the other two bullies simultaneously.

"What are you talking about?" said Kipper. He unlocked his locker and opened it up.

"HEY! WHAT THE HECK IS THIS?!!?"
Kipper screamed. "SOMEBODY'S BEEN IN
MY LOCKER!!!"

Loogie, Bugg, and Finkstein saw the Susie
Sunshine Friendship Bracelet Kit and shook
their heads in disgust.

Kipper kicked the kit into the hallway and
stomped on it. Then he tore open his duffel
bag. It was empty.

"AAAAUGH!" Kipper screamed.
"SOMEBODY *STOLE* ALL MY MONEY!"

Kipper looked up and down the hall
frantically. "When I find out who's been in
my locker, I'm gonna . . . I'm gonna . . ."

"*Kiss* them?" asked Finkstein. The other
two bullies laughed.

Kipper grabbed Finkstein by his shirt collar and shook him back and forth like a rag doll. "WHAT ARE YOU TALKING ABOUT?!!?" he screamed.

"This!" said Finkstein. He showed Kipper the text that had been sent from Kipper's phone.

"I-I-I DIDN'T WRITE THAT!!!" Kipper screamed.

"Well, what's up with those friendship bracelets on your wrist, then?" asked Bugg.

"The—the cheerleaders gave me those!" said Kipper

At that very moment, a group of cheerleaders was coming in from practice outside.

"I'll prove it!" said Kipper. He showed the bracelets to the cheerleaders, waving his wrist at them like a lunatic. "You guys made these for me, right?" Kipper asked them, pointing desperately at the friendship bracelets.

The cheerleaders gave Kipper a strange look. "Eeeeww," said Wendy Swan, the head cheerleader.

Kipper blinked his eyes like a crazy person. He began breathing heavily. He clenched his fists and shook with rage. Kipper's friends glanced at each other, exchanging silent, worried looks. They each took a few steps backward, as if they feared Kipper might explode.

"Hey, uh, we'll see you later, *Susie Sunshine*," said Loogie.

The three bullies walked away laughing, leaving Kipper alone and frenzied.

Finally, Kipper returned to his locker. He grabbed his phone and found an envelope beside it.

Kipper tore the envelope open with insane rage and read the note inside.

CHAPTER 19
WHO IS WEDGIE MAGEE?

George and Harold stopped by the thrift store on their way home to buy a bunch of supplies for Tuesday. The checkout lady gave them a very strange look as they walked up to the cash register.

"What are all these dresses for?" asked the lady.

"They're for school," said Harold.

"Oh," said the lady.

When they got home, the two boys sat in George's bedroom and counted Kipper's stolen money. It totaled $916.00.

"I feel like Robin Hood!" said George. "What should we do with all this dough?"

"I think we should use it to buy lunches for all the kindergartners!" said Harold. "That's what it was supposed to be used for in the first place!"

George agreed. He picked up the phone and called the Piqua Pizza Palace. "Can you guys deliver pizzas to the elementary school around noon tomorrow?" he said. "Really? Awesome! We'll take five large cheese pizzas, five large pepperoni, and five large black olive and pineapple." George discussed the details and arranged to drop off the payment in the morning. "We're all set for lunch tomorrow," said George.

"Cool!" said Harold.

The next morning on the way to school,
George and Harold walked by the Piqua Pizza
Palace. It wouldn't open until 11:00 A.M., but
that didn't matter. George took out an envelope
filled with money, coupons, instructions, and
a tip for the delivery guy, and dropped it
through the mail slot on the front door.

George and Harold had a very busy day
ahead of them. They got to school early and
unlocked the door to their secret restroom
stall. As the two boys unloaded their supplies
and arranged their stilts, they heard the
sounds of the other students beginning to
arrive. Today *sounded* just like any other day,
but things at Jerome Horwitz Elementary
School were starting to change.

Kipper stood by the entrance of the school like normal, but he wasn't just stealing money from the kindergartners like he usually did. Today he also wanted information. He seemed a little anxious, and shaky—like he hadn't gotten a lot of sleep the night before. Kipper's three buddies (who usually stuck close to his side) were keeping their distance from him. Loogie, Bugg, and Finkstein all watched Kipper with worried looks on their faces.

Kipper grabbed every kid who came toward the door and asked them all the same question:

"Who is Wedgie Magee?"

Nobody outside the school had ever heard of Wedgie Magee. But inside the school, George and Harold were busy spreading rumors about this mysterious stranger.

"Did you hear about Wedgie Magee?" George asked Harold loudly near a group of gossipy girls.

"Yeah!" said Harold, even louder. "I heard Wedgie Magee is a *GHOST*!"

"Me, too!" said George. "I heard Wedgie Magee haunts the hallways of this very school, looking for REVENGE!"

"Revenge against who?" asked Harold intensely.

"Against Kipper Krupp!" cried George in a booming whisper.

The gossipy girls listened closely as George continued. "I heard that Kipper Krupp got *CURSED* by the ghost of Wedgie Magee!"

"Heavens, no!" cried Harold. "What for?"

"For being mean to kindergartners!" said George. "Wedgie Magee is the patron ghost of kindergartners!"

"I did not know that," said Harold. "Oh, poor Kipper! Poor, *poor* Kipper!"

George and Harold walked away, shaking their heads with pity. The wide-eyed group of gossipy girls had been rendered uncharacteristically speechless. Quickly, they began sending frantic texts to all of their friends about the horrible ghost of Wedgie Magee.

Within an hour, the whole school knew the terrible truth about Wedgie Magee, and it didn't take long before the information made its way to Kipper and his friends.

"That's *stupid*!" said Kipper. "There's no such thing as ghosts!"

"Y-Yeah," said Loogie, "but I heard he can go through walls and even lockers! Maybe the ghost stole all of that money yesterday!"

"That's a bunch of *BUNK*!" said Kipper. "What's a ghost gonna do with money?"

"M-M-Maybe he'll give it back to the kindergartners!" said Finkstein. "I heard Wedgie Magee was a friend to all kindergartners!"

"Uh, excuse me," said a pizza delivery guy
holding fifteen large pizza boxes. "I'm supposed
to deliver these pizzas to the kindergartners.
Do you guys know where the cafeteria is?"

"Down the hall," said Kipper. "Hey, who
ordered those pizzas?"

"I don't know," said the delivery guy. "I
never saw him. I think his name was *Wedgie*
something."

Kipper gasped. "Y-You say you never saw him?"

"Nope!" said the delivery guy. "*Nobody's* ever
seen him. But he's a pretty good tipper!"

CHAPTER 20

TUESDAY AFTERNOON

Lunchtime was a great success. All the kindergartners loved their pizza and pop, and nobody seemed to mind that it had all been bought and paid for by a ghost.

"Haunted pizza tastes the best!" said Freddie Moore, and the other kindergartners couldn't have agreed more.

After school, Kipper unlocked his locker
and once again put his padlock on top of the
locker. And just like yesterday, George pulled
on the long strip of paper, switching Kipper's
padlock for their own.

Kipper grabbed George and Harold's
padlock, clicked it closed on his locker, and
pulled hard to make sure it was really locked
tightly. It was.

Once the hallways were empty, George and Harold got back to work. George unlocked Kipper's locker while Harold filled it up with pretty lacy dresses, making sure their bows looked beautiful and their ruffles were just right. George typed another text on Kipper's phone and left a new envelope beside it. Then they locked the door with Kipper's lock and set everything up so it would work again the same way tomorrow.

"Are you sure we can't stay here and watch all the fun?" asked Harold.

"We better not," said George. "Things are about to get even *uglier*!"

CHAPTER 21
THINGS GET EVEN UGLIER

When wrestling practice ended at 4:30, Kipper's friends rushed to their lockers and turned on their phones. As they had suspected, there was another text from Kipper.

Oct 23, 3:41 PM

Lets play
Princess!
I got pritty
dresses 4 U 2
try on after
practiss.
XOXOXOXO

By the time Kipper got to his locker, he knew something was wrong.

"What?" he yelled at his friends. "What *NOW?"*

"Sorry, dude," said Loogie, "but we don't wanna play *dress up* with you!"

"Yeah, *Princess*," said Finkstein. The three bullies chuckled.

Kipper grabbed Bugg's phone and read the message.

"I-I DID NOT WRITE THIS!" Kipper yelled. "And I DON'T have any *DRESSES* in my locker, either! I can *PROVE* it!"

Kipper unlocked his locker and opened the door . . .

. . . revealing three of the prettiest dresses anyone had ever seen.

Kipper's friends started laughing as he closed the door and checked to make sure he had opened the right locker.

"*SOMEBODY* IS MESSING WITH ME," screamed Kipper. He tore the dresses out of his locker and whipped them to the floor.

"Maybe you're just getting in touch with your feminine side," said Loogie. Kipper's three friends burst into hysterical laughter.

"Laugh it up, chumps!" yelled Kipper, as he searched the top shelf of his locker. Sure enough, there was another envelope. He ripped it open and read the message out loud:

THERE IS NO ESCAPE!
Signed, Wedgie Magee

Kipper's friends stopped laughing and looked at the note.

"Dude," said Bugg, "I think you really DID get cursed!"

"At least it's a funny curse," said Loogie.

CHAPTER 22
WEDNESDAY

Another day, another awesome lunch for George and Harold and their classmates. The Piqua Pizza Palace had even delivered salads and breadsticks, and the kindergartners had never been happier.

At the end of the day, when wrestling practice was over, Kipper's three friends dashed back to their lockers as fast as they could to see what bizarre thing Kipper was going to do next. They were not disappointed.

4:31 PM

FROM Kipper Krupp

U R invitid 2 my pritty dolly tea party. IF U need 2 borow a dolly, meet me @ my Locker. I GoT Xtras!!! XOXO

Reply   Send

Kipper was already angry when he reached his locker. He knew something was not right.

"What?" he yelled at his friends. "WHAT ARE YOU GUYS LAUGHING ABOUT?!!?"

"Dude," said Loogie, "can I bring a teddy bear to your tea party, or is it just for dollies only?" The three bullies busted up laughing.

Kipper grabbed Loogie's phone and read the message.

"I — DID — NOT — WRITE — THIS!" Kipper screamed wildly. "And I DON'T have any DOLLS in my locker, either!"

Kipper grabbed the key from the chain around his neck, unlocked his padlock, and threw the locker door open with a mighty crash.

About twenty dolls tumbled out of the locker and fell into a pile at Kipper's feet.

Kipper's friends each took a few steps back. They weren't sure whether to keep laughing or start running. Kipper did nothing at first. He just stood there looking down at the mountain of dolls at his feet.

Then he began breathing heavily as he started to twitch. The trembling originated at Kipper's feet, making its way slowly up his legs. By the time it reached Kipper's upper body, he was shaking like a volcano that was about to explode. Kipper squeezed his fists into tight knots of fury as he raised his right foot and began kicking the dolls.

"I HATE YOU! I HATE YOU! I HATE YOU!" Kipper screamed, as he punted his pretty dollies up and down the hallway.

Kipper's friends had never seen a freak-out quite like this. Kipper grabbed two of the bigger dolls and started swinging them around and around, smashing them against his locker door and just about anything

else that was nearby. Then came the tearing and the biting and the stomping and the decapitating. Loogie, Bugg, and Finkstein decided it might be a good time to start running.

Kipper's berserk-a-thon lasted about fifteen minutes. Finally, he collapsed, exhausted, in a pile of fluffy polyester filling, shredded dolly dresses, and tiny plastic arms, legs, and heads. Kipper just sat there, breathing slowly for a long time and staring at nothing. Then, Kipper thought of something. It was as if he had finally figured out the mysteries of the ages.

He stood up and grabbed his padlock from the top of his locker. Carefully, he turned it over and over again in his hands, studying it very closely.

"A-*HA*!" he exclaimed.

CHAPTER 23
THURSDAY

Things were back to normal on Thursday. Kipper stood in front of the school and made every kindergartner hand over their lunch money. "Things are gonna change around here," Kipper told the children. "Starting tomorrow, your taxes are going UP! You kids are gonna have to pay me four bucks a day, or it's *WEDGIE TIME*!"

Kipper's three friends watched the shakedowns from a distance. Finally, they approached Kipper nervously.

"Dude," said Loogie. "What are you doing, man?"

"I'm taking back what's rightfully *MINE*!" said Kipper.

"But aren't you afraid of the ghost of Wedgie Magee?" asked Bugg.

"There is no ghost of Wedgie Magee, you moron!" yelled Kipper. "It's all a setup! I figured it out last night! Somebody has been

picking my padlock and putting stuff in my locker!"

"But who would do that?" asked Loogie.

"The same person who has been writing those stupid texts on my phone!" said Kipper. "But it's all going to end today!"

"How?" asked Loogie.

"I got a NEW padlock!" said Kipper. He reached into his pocket and pulled out a brand-new Supa-Doopa Combo Lock 2000. "This thing is totally *pick-proof*," said Kipper.

The four fiends walked into the school and headed for the lockers. Kipper unlocked his old padlock and threw it into the garbage can, along with the key around his sweaty neck. Then Kipper put his all-new *pick-proof* combination padlock on his locker and clicked it shut.

"Let's see somebody try to mess with me NOW!" Kipper sneered.

At noon, when the pizza delivery guy showed up with lunch for the kindergartners, Kipper stopped him in the hallway.

"We'll take those pizzas," said Kipper.

"But I'm supposed to deliver them to the kindergartners," said the delivery guy.

"We'll do it for you," said Kipper.

"Sorry," said the delivery guy, "but I've got strict instructions from Wedgie Magee to—"

"Oh, Uncle Benny!" Kipper yelled.

Mr. Krupp came bounding up the hallway.

Boom! Boom! Boom! Boom! Boom!

"What seems to be the problem, Kipper?" he asked.

"This guy is delivering pizzas to the kindergartners," said Kipper. "Is he *allowed* to do that?"

"Absolutely NOT," said Principal Krupp. "Those kids are on diets!"

"See?" said Kipper to the delivery guy. "Now *gimme* those!"

Kipper's crew took the pizzas and the pop away from the delivery guy. They brought it straight to the kindergartners' table in the cafeteria and started stuffing their faces.

"*MMMMMM!*" said Kipper to the hungry kindergartners. "This pizza sure is *tasty*!" The four barbarians devoured eight whole pizzas between them and finished off fourteen cans of pop. Then they sold all of their leftovers to some of the other students.

"Too bad the *KINDERGARTNERS* can't buy any." Kipper laughed. "But they don't have any money, do they?"

George and Harold were heartbroken. They had already seen Kipper's new padlock and noticed that it never left Kipper's hands when he unlocked it — not even for a second.

"Well," said Harold sadly, "I guess the jig is up!"

"Nothing's over 'til *WE* say it's over," said George. "We've got to think of something else — *and quick!*"

CHAPTER 24
FOAMY, WHITE ECTOPLASM

After school, George and Harold waited until the hallways were empty. Then they opened their secret stall in the boys' restroom. George had an idea. He climbed up on the stilts, and Harold pulled the pants all the way up to the top of George's head. Then George tried walking around, looking out the zipper hole with one eye.

"Well," said George. "How do I look?"

"I'm not sure," said Harold. "You kinda look like an afro with legs."

"Hmmmm . . ." said George, as he peeked at himself in the bathroom mirror. "I think I'm going to need a haircut!" George's idea would have to wait until tomorrow.

Fortunately, the two boys had a backup plan. George and Harold ran to the convenience store up the street and bought four cans of shaving cream and a box of bendy straws. Then they hurried back to the school.

"We're gonna have to work fast," said Harold. The two boys opened their box of bendy straws and pushed a straw over the spray nozzle of each can of shaving cream. Then George stuck a straw up Kipper's locker vent and began spraying.

Harold took another can, stuck the straw up the vent of Loogie's locker, and started squirting.

After a few minutes, George's and Harold's cans were empty. They then took two more cans and did the same thing to Bugg's and Finkstein's lockers.

George and Harold hid the empty shaving cream cans in their secret restroom stall. Then they ran out the back door of the school toward the football field, screaming their heads off.

The cheerleaders, who were just finishing their practice, saw George and Harold running around like lunatics. "What's wrong, little boys?" asked one of the cheerleaders.

"W-W-W-We just saw a g-g-g-ghost!" cried
George.

"Y-Y-Yeah!" cried Harold. "He was in the
hallway over by the lockers!"

The cheerleaders were frightened. "What
did he look like?" they asked.

"He was invisible," cried George. "But he
left a trail of foamy, white ectoplasm wherever
he went!"

The cheerleaders screamed. They were
terrified, but they were also very curious.

The girls huddled together in a tight, shivering group as they tiptoed into the school to see for themselves. Everything looked normal, but they still screamed a lot anyway. One of them pushed the button on the drinking fountain, and when water squirted out, they all screamed some more.

"What's going on?" yelled Kipper, who had just gotten out of wrestling practice with his buddies.

The cheerleaders screamed again. "Th-Th-There's a ghost up here!" cried Wendy Swan. "Some little kids saw it! It was leaving foamy, white ectoplasm everywhere."

"That's crazy!" Kipper yelled. "Ghosts aren't for real!" He and his buddies laughed arrogantly as they unlocked their lockers and opened the doors.

Suddenly, four giant waves of foamy, white shaving cream splashed out into the hallway.

"FOAMY, WHITE ECTOPLASM!" yelled the cheerleaders. They screamed and ran for their lives.

"*Ectoplasm?*" cried Bugg. "I've heard of that! Th-Th-That's *ghost juice*!"

"I-I-I got *ghost juice* on my pants!" Loogie wailed, as he burst into tears.

"Get it OFF! Get it OFF! *Get it OFF!*" screamed Finkstein, as he jumped around spastically swatting at the shaving cream that covered his legs. *"I HATE GHOST JUICE!!!"*

"THERE'S
NO SUCH THING AS
GHOSTS!" Kipper yelled,
but it was no use. Loogie,
Bugg, and Finkstein slammed
their lockers and screamed in horror
as they slipped and slid in the foamy, white
ectoplasm. The three petrified pests tumbled
down the stairs, tripping and pushing and
elbowing each other as they struggled to glide
out the front door.

Kipper was at his wit's end. He plopped
down on the floor in the middle of the hallway
and curled up into a shivering ball.

"UNCLE BENNY!" he wailed.

As usual, Mr. Krupp came running down
the hallway.

Boom! Boom! Boom! Boom! Boom!

"What's wrong? What's wrong?" yelled
Mr. Krupp.

Kipper showed Mr. Krupp the ectoplasm
and told him the whole terrifying story.

"That's a bunch of *BUNK*!" yelled Mr. Krupp. "This isn't ectoplasm, it's shaving cream! I use this same brand myself!"

"Shaving cream?" said Kipper. "B-But how did it get inside our lockers?"

"Well, somebody probably sprayed it through those vents on the door!" Mr. Krupp said. "It's the oldest trick in the book!"

Kipper studied the vents on the locker door as his passive, fearful expression slowly turned into a venomous visage of violence. Now Kipper was *REALLY* mad.

CHAPTER 25
THURSDAY AFTERNOON

That afternoon at Harold's house, George and Harold wrote and illustrated a brand-new comic book. When they were done, they scanned each page and printed out four copies on Harold's printer.

The comic book had to look very old, so
they took a large bowl outside and filled it
with water. Harold added two handfuls of dirt
and stirred eight tablespoons of instant coffee
crystals into the water. George carefully tore
the edges of each page, then crumpled them
all up into little balls and soaked them in the
giant bowl of filthy water.

Once each page was completely soaked, the two friends carefully clipped them up in the garage so they could dry overnight.

"What on earth are you boys doing?" said Harold's mother.

"It's for school," said Harold.

"Oh," said Harold's mom.

Next, the two boys went back inside Harold's house.

"Now we've gotta order some pizzas!" said George.

"Order pizzas?" cried Harold. "Why? Kipper's just going to steal them again!"

"That's what I'm counting on," George said with a devilish grin.

George picked up the telephone and spoke with the manager of Piqua Pizza Palace.

"I'd like to order four pizzas for tomorrow," said George. "What's the hottest kind of chili peppers you guys have? *Ghost* chili peppers? Hmmmm. Can we get *double* ghost chili peppers on each pizza? Cool!"

After the pizzas were ordered, it was time for George's haircut. Harold went to the closet and found the clippers and scissors his mom always used to cut his hair. Harold had never cut anybody's hair before, but he was more than happy to give it a try.

"Just make the top part flat," said George. "So it won't stick out when I wear those stilt pants!"

"I'll do my best," said Harold.

Harold clipped and cut, then he snipped
and shaped. When he was done, George
looked at himself in the mirror.

"I LOOK *AWESOME*!" George exclaimed.
"I'm gonna wear my hair like this from
now on!"

And he always did.

CHAPTER 26
WHEN KIPPER GETS ANGRY—REALLY, REALLY ANGRY

The next morning, George and Harold's comic book pages were dry enough to staple together. George sprinkled each page with baby powder to make them look dusty and prehistoric.

"Man," said Harold. "These look like they came from the 1980s or something!"

Friday morning at school was turning out to be the worst day ever. All week long, George and Harold had worked to make things better for their fellow kindergartners, but they had only succeeded in turning Kipper and his gang into MONSTERS.

Kipper had told his friends about the shaving-cream prank, and now they were really, really angry, too. The four bullies knew somebody was pranking them, and they were going to make every kindergartner's life intolerable until they found out who it was.

"HEY! Where's my eight dollars?" Kipper yelled at Donny Shoemyer, who happened to be the first kindergartner he saw on Friday morning.

"I-I thought you said *four* dollars," said Donny.

"I did," said Kipper. "But taxes just went up *again*. And they're gonna stay high until I find out the name of the person who's been pulling pranks on me!"

"I-I-I don't know who it is," said Donny.

"Well, you'd better find out," Kipper growled. "Or I'm gonna stop being such a nice guy to you little twerps!" Kipper grabbed Donny's money while his creepy companions gave Donny the worst wedgie of his life.

"You owe me four more dollars!" yelled Kipper. "So bring *TWELVE* dollars on Monday, or you're gonna wish you'd never been born!"

The rest of the kindergartners received similar treatment when they tried to enter the school. Unfortunately for them, nobody had any idea who was pranking Kipper and his friends.

At lunchtime, the delivery guy from Piqua Pizza Palace showed up.

"Hey!" shouted Kipper. "How come there's only four pizzas today?"

"That's all Mr. Magee ordered," said the delivery guy.

"What a *cheapskate*!" Kipper sneered. "Well, hand 'em over, bub!"

"OK, but I need to give you a warning," said the delivery guy. "These pizzas are really, REALLY HOT."

"They'd *better* be hot!" yelled Kipper. "I *hate* cold pizza!"

Kipper yanked the pizzas out of the
delivery guy's hands and headed toward the
cafeteria with his friends. They kicked the
lunchroom door open and strutted over to
the kindergartners' table.

"MMMMM! Look at all the tasty pizza we
got!" Kipper said to the hungry kids. "I'll bet
you guys are *starving*! Awww, that's so sad."

Kipper, Bugg, Loogie, and Finkstein each
grabbed a giant slice and crammed it into
their mouths. The four bullies smiled
obnoxiously as they chewed with wide,
revoltingly cavernous mouths that showed
every mushy glob of shiny, doughy goo.

"Whew! This pizza's kinda hot," said Finkstein, as he swallowed harshly and wiped some sweat off his forehead.

"Y-Yeah," said Loogie. "This pizza is *really* HOT!"

"Ow! Ow! Owowowowow!" cried Kipper. "This pizza is WAY TOO HOT!!!"

"It BURNS! It BURNS!" wailed Bugg, as he stuck out his tongue and tried to blow on it. "Ooo! OOOO! *OOOOOOOO!*"

Suddenly, the bullies' exaggerated smiles morphed into bug-eyed expressions of sheer horror. Quickly, they began wiping off their tongues with their filthy hands, but it was too late. The ghost chilis had already done their damage. Kipper and his terror-stricken buddies stampeded to the drinking fountain, waving their arms and shrieking like a cackle of panicked hyenas. They pushed and shoved each other in a desperate attempt to splash cold water onto their tongues.

Kipper wasn't having much success at the drinking fountain, so he bolted to the milk table. There, he began clawing the tiny half-pint milk cartons open, one after the other, and splashing the milk into his face. The other three bullies followed, shoving and jabbing and kicking each other as they tore the tiny cartons with their teeth and sprayed the milk into their gaping, smoldering mouths.

When the milk was gone, the four bullies
dropped to the floor, grunting and wailing and
crying for their mommies as they licked up
all the milk that had spilled during their
lacto-guzzling frenzy. The entire event had
been filmed by about twenty kids on their
phones, and the embarrassing videos were all
posted online before the end of lunch period.

Kipper, Bugg, Loogie, and Finkstein all
spent the next two hours in the nurse's room,
holding ice packs on their tongues and crying
like toddlers. They started to feel better just
as the school day was ending and wrestling
practice was about to begin.

228

CHAPTER 27
SOMETHING WEDGIE
THIS WAY COMES

At 2:45 P.M., when the final bell rang, George
and Harold ran to their secret restroom stall
and grabbed two empty glass jelly jars. Then
they headed out toward the groundskeeper's
shed.

There were always a ton of spiders back
there, and George and Harold worked very
hard to safely capture as many as they could.

"We gotta hurry," said George. "It looks
like it's going to rain!"

Once they had collected about twenty
harmless garden spiders each, they ran back
upstairs to the lockers in the empty hallway.

Harold held a piece of paper under one of
the lower vent slots of Kipper's locker. George
opened his glass jelly jar and sprinkled some
spiders onto the paper as Harold blew softly.
About ten spiders gently slid across the paper
and through the slot, disappearing into the
darkened depths of Kipper's locker. Next they
moved on to Loogie's, Bugg's, and Finkstein's
lockers, gently blowing an assortment of eight-
legged residents into their vents, too.

George and Harold knew that it takes about an hour for a spider to build a completed web. They looked at the clock on the wall and realized they had only forty-four minutes until wrestling practice was over.

"I hope those spiders work fast," said Harold.

"We gotta work fast, too," said George. "There's still lots of stuff to be done!"

The two boys grabbed some supplies and sneaked into the boys' locker room next to the gym. Harold found Kipper's deodorant stick, pulled off the cap, and twisted the dial on the bottom until the deodorant stuck all the way out of the canister. George pulled the thick, white deodorant off and threw it into the garbage can.

Then he opened a package of extra-spicy jalapeño cream cheese and began packing it into the plastic deodorant canister with a spoon.

When the canister was filled, Harold molded the cream cheese into shape with his fingers, then popped the cap back on. George put the deodorant back in Kipper's gym locker next to his soap and his towel, while Harold started working on Loogie's deodorant. It took about thirty minutes, but soon George and Harold had transformed all four of the bullies' deodorant sticks into jalapeño cream cheese applicators.

Once everything was back where it belonged, George and Harold rushed to their secret stall in the boys' restroom. Time was running out.

George climbed onto his stilts as Harold gathered the ancient-looking comics and an old walkie-talkie. Quickly, the two friends sneaked out to the hallway and got to work.

Harold slid a comic book through one of the lower vent slots of each bully's locker while George placed the walkie-talkie on top of the lockers and pumped up the volume. They finished just as wrestling practice ended.

Dark clouds were beginning to gather outside, and a distant thunder could be heard rumbling miles away. A terrible storm was coming.

Meanwhile, back in the locker room, Kipper and his cohorts changed their clothes, smeared on some deodorant, and strutted out to their lockers. Lightning was beginning to flash outside, filling the school windows with crackling bursts of fluorescence.

The four hooligans unlocked their locker doors and swung them open, just as a deafening thunderclap rocked the school hallway.

CRASH!!!

The terror-stricken tyrants stared in horrified astonishment at their spiderweb-caked compartments.

Loogie, who had a severely intense fear of spiders, was the first one to freak out.

"L-L-L-Lockers! H-H-H-Haunted! S-S-S-Spiders!" was all he could manage to verbalize as an earsplitting smash of thunder rattled the school. The four ruffians shrieked in panic.

Loogie was losing it. He flicked his hands wildly as he stood in place, leaning from side to side, impulsively raising one knee to his chest, and then the other. "We gotta get out of here, dudes!" he sobbed. "Seriously, we gotta get out of here, dudes. *SERIOUSLY,* DUDES! We *GOTTA* get out of here! DUDES!!! *DUDES!!!*"

"Just a doggone minute," Kipper protested. "What's this?" He reached carefully into his web-choked locker and pulled out an ancient-looking comic book.

"I don't know," said Finkstein. "But I got one, too."

"Me, too," said Bugg.

Loogie would have added that he also had one in his locker, but he had become too frightened to speak. All he could manage was short bursts of screams as he danced around the hallway, twitching and jerking like a demented chicken.

Kipper opened the antique comic and began to read aloud as turbulent thunder rumbled around them.

CHAPTER 28

The CUrse OF Wedgie Magee
(a true storie)

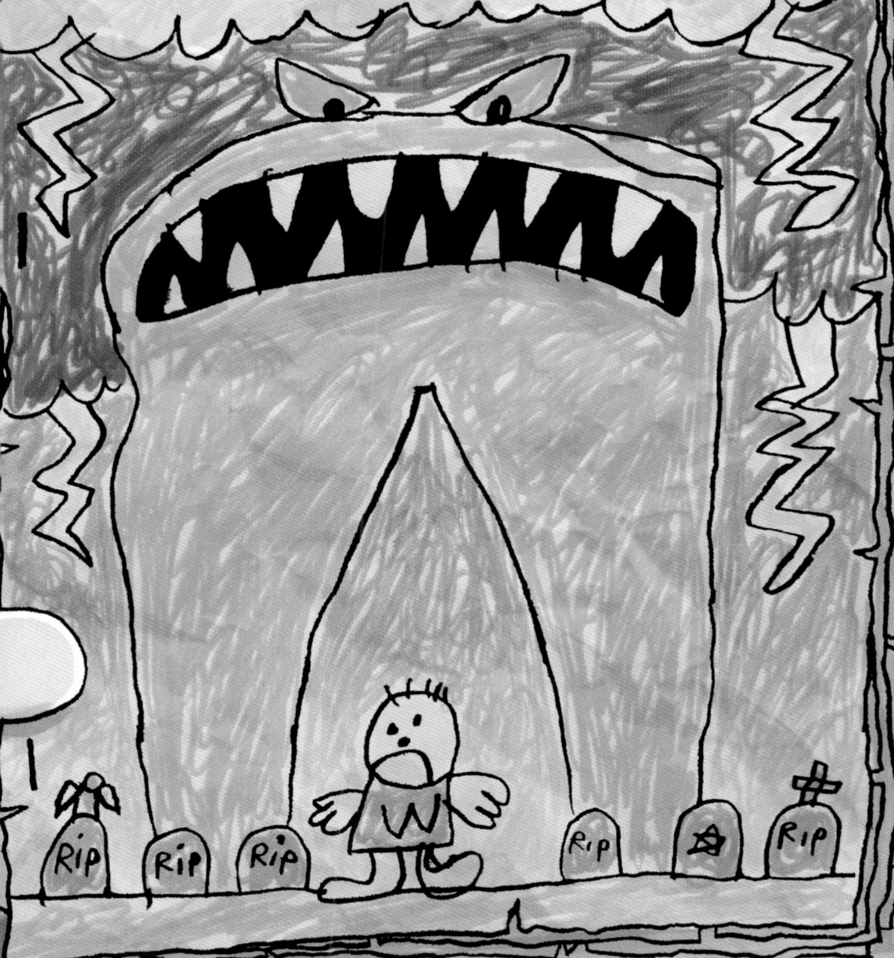

The next Day The BULLYS came BY

Its Time For your Wedgie!

no way!

wedgie Mag-ee Pored The po shen on his Pants

But Then

OH NO

SSSSS SS

His Pants disapered

BONIS SECKSHON

★ HOW TO TELL IF YOU ★
   GOT CURSED:

① YOU START ACKTING ALL
   WEERD AND STUFF.

② YOU WANT TO PLAY WITH
   DOLLYS AND DRESSES AND
   ~~FRENDSHIP~~ BRASELITS.

③ YOU GET ECKTOPLASIM ON
   YOUR STUFF (AND SPIDERS TOO).

④ AWESOME FOOD LIKE PIZZA
   TASTS ALL HOT AND BURNS
   YOUR MOUTH AND STUFF.

⑤ YOUR ~~AND~~ ARMPITS GET ~~AND~~
   ALL BURNY AND STUFF.

HOW TO UNDO THIS CURSE

YOU MUST UNDO ALL THE BAD
STUFF YOU DID AND NEVER ~~~~
PICK ON NOBODY EVER AGAIN!

CHAPTER 29
THE PERFECT STORM

It was getting dark now, and the storm outside was intensifying.

The four bullies stared in knee-melting terror at the dusty, ancient comic in Kipper's trembling hands. Their mouths hung open in shock, but they were too afraid to move.

Finally, Finkstein began spastically scratching his sweat-soaked armpits.

"Dudes," he blurted, "we're *DEAD*, man. It's *OVER*!! Game OVER, man!"

Bugg began to cry. "My *pits* are burning, man," he sobbed. "I think I got *the curse*!"

"M-M-M-Me, too," Loogie squeaked, as tears poured down his face.

Kipper looked into the quivering eyes of his three terrified friends. His armpits were burning as well, but he was too frightened to admit it.

Suddenly, a deafening blast of thunder shook the building. The lightbulbs in the school flickered twice, and the bullies held each other and sobbed uncontrollably.

Inside the restroom, George and Harold could hear their arch-enemies shrieking out in the hallway, and the two friends tried as hard as they could to keep from laughing. They both knew if they started, they'd never be able to stop. Harold picked up his walkie-talkie and pressed the "transmit" button.

The toy walkie-talkie on top of the lockers clicked with a crackle of static.

"I am the haunted pants of Wedgie Magee!" whispered Harold over the tiny speaker.

"HEY!" cried Kipper. "DID—DID YOU GUYS HEAR THAT?"

"I am coming for yoooooooou!" Harold whispered.

"No! No! No! No! No! No! NOOOO!" screamed Loogie, who was now running around in small circles, punching his head with his fists (for some strange reason).

Lightning exploded again, and the hallways rumbled with thunder. The four bullies had now become completely unhinged. Bugg dropped to the floor and curled up into a shivering ball, crying out for his mother to come and save him.

"L-L-LEAVE US ALONE," Kipper screamed, swinging his fists in the air. "WE'RE *SORRY*!"

Mr. Krupp was in the middle of a teachers' meeting all the way on the other end of the building when he heard the screaming.

"It sounds like Kipper's freaking out again," he growled, slamming his fist on the table. "And I'm going to get to the bottom of it!" He got up from the meeting and stomped out of the room.

Kipper and his friends heard the pounding sounds of stomping feet coming from the other side of the school building. **Boom!** *Boom!* **Boom!** *Boom!* **Boom!** *Boom!* **Boom!** *Boom!* **Boom!** *Boom!* The stomping got louder and louder, and closer and closer.

"Let's hide in the bathroom!" screamed Loogie, through his tears. Immediately, the four frightened friends scrambled for the bathroom door.

Inside the bathroom, George and Harold were still getting ready for their final prank. Harold steadied the wooden stilts while George pulled the tall pair of pants up over his head. The two kindergartners didn't know they were about to be ambushed.

"I can't see," said George.

"Here," said Harold. "Let me—"

Suddenly, the restroom door crashed open and the terrified bullies tumbled inside. They looked at Harold holding on to the giant pair of pants in front of them. Lightning pierced the darkened clouds, and everyone froze. The stomping footsteps came closer and closer. **Boom!** *Boom!* **Boom!** *Boom!* **Boom!** *Boom!* **Boom!** *Boom!*

"W-W-What are you doing with those *pants*, kid?" cried Kipper.

Harold couldn't think of a thing to say. It wasn't supposed to happen like this. They weren't ready. For a split second, Harold saw his entire life flash before his eyes. He and George were going to get caught. Their lives were about to end. The footsteps in the hallway got even louder.

Boom! *Boom!* **Boom!** *Boom!* **Boom!** *Boom!*

George knew they were in trouble. He couldn't see, but he grasped the stilts anyway and took a blind, wobbly step forward. The bullies beheld what appeared to be a pair of pants walking by themselves. They grasped each other and shrieked in earsplitting horror.

"Get away from those pants, kid," cried Bugg. *"GET AWAY FROM THOSE PANTS!"*

Then, as if an angel had whispered it into his ear, Harold thought of the perfect thing to say.

"What pants?" he asked.

BOOM!

Suddenly, time seemed to stand still.

BOOM!

The four bullies stepped back in horror.

BOOM!

Their eyes grew impossibly wide.

BOOM!

They opened their mouths to scream . . .

BOOM!

. . . but not a sound came out.

BOOM!

George took another step toward the bullies . . .

BOOM!

. . . as they clawed at the wall behind them.

BOOM!

Then the lightning flashed again . . .

. . . and everything went dark.

The terrible storm had knocked out a

power line nearby, and the school was now

completely black. Kipper and his crew

scrambled over each other, desperately trying

to make their way through the restroom door.

Mr. Krupp was to be their next obstacle.

He had finally reached the lockers when the

lights went out. His elephantine footsteps had

stopped cold, and he stood in the darkness,

breathing heavily and sweating abundantly.

When the four squealing derelicts finally

tumbled out of the restroom and bolted down

the dark hallway, they smashed right into him.

Nobody would be able to blame the bullies

for what they did next. In their profoundly

petrified perceptions, they must have believed

that Mr. Krupp was some kind of giant, wet,

fleshy monster—and they treated him as

such. Screeching and wailing in the darkness,

they kicked and clobbered the warm, wet, bulbous

creature with all the strength they had.

The four distressed delinquents then tumbled down the stairs and shoved their way through the back door of the school. As they ran across the football field toward their homes, something about Kipper and his friends changed forever. They would never again be the same despicable bullies they once were.

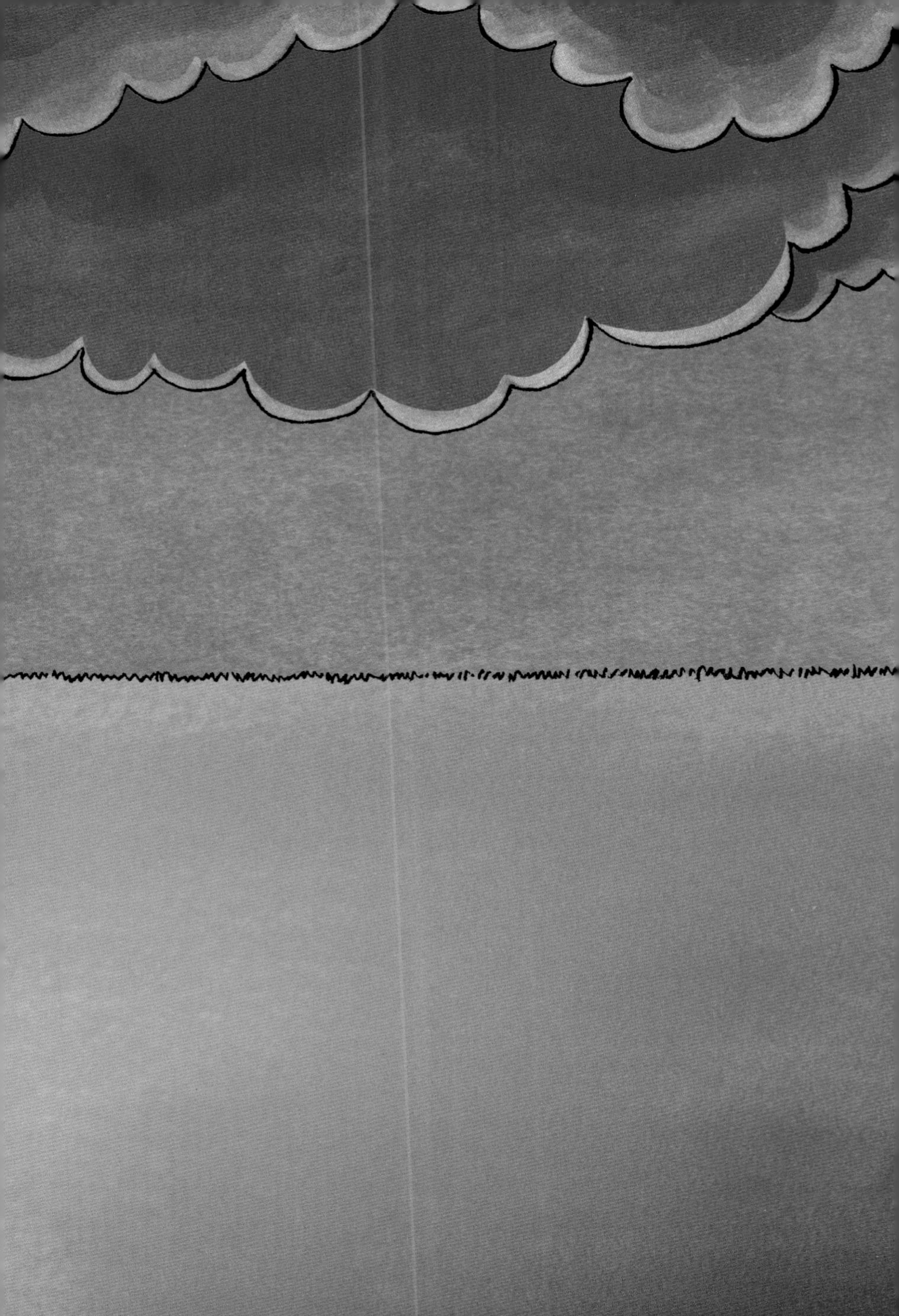

CHAPTER 30
THE WONDERFUL, HAPPY, INCREDIBLY DELIGHTFUL ENDING

Monday morning was a very stressful time for Donny Shoemyer. He had not been able to scrape up the twelve dollars he owed Kipper, so he was trying to sneak into the school through the back door without being noticed. Kipper saw him.

"Hey, kid!" yelled Kipper. "Wait up! I got something for ya!"

Donny pulled at the door, but it was locked. He kept pulling and pulling anyway as Kipper approached.

"I got some money for you," said Kipper nervously. He reached into his pocket and handed Donny a crinkled five dollar bill.

Donny stopped pulling at the door and looked at the money in Kipper's hand. "Is this a trick?" Donny asked.

"No," Kipper said. "I'm really sorry I took money from you, kid. I'm gonna pay ya back every dollar as soon as I can, OK?"

"Umm . . . OK," said Donny. He took the five dollar bill from Kipper's hand and rushed to the front door of the school. His morning had turned out a *LOT* different than he had expected.

All around the school, the other kindergartners were having similar experiences.

Finkstein was not only passing out money, he was also offering to carry every kindergartner's book bag to class. Bugg was handing out cash and free bubble gum, and Loogie was distributing dollars AND letting the kindergartners give him as many wedgies as they wanted.

Line STARTS
HERE

Free
WEDGiES
(hiLe Supplies Last)

Kipper and his three friends eventually paid back all the money they had stolen, and they never bullied another person for as long as they lived.

Once George and Harold were certain that their enemies had truly been reformed, they called off the vengeful wrath of Wedgie Magee. The terrifying curse had finally been lifted, everyone was happy, and all was well with the world.

I'd like to tell you that this is the end of our story. I really would—but I can't. Because this wonderful, happy, incredibly delightful ending is what was *supposed* to happen . . . not what actually *did* happen.

Remember back in chapter 8 when Tippy Tinkletrousers was fighting Captain Underpants and he accidentally froze his giant Robo-Legs to the school's football field? Well, if you'll recall, Tippy got out of this jam by zapping himself back in time exactly five years earlier.

Now, see if you can guess which night occurred exactly *five years earlier*. If you guessed the night of the terrible thunderstorm that forever changed the lives of Kipper and his buddies, you'd be correct.

Unfortunately, by some wild and tragic coincidence, Tippy sent himself and his gigantic Robo-Pants back in time to the very moment when Kipper and his friends were running across the football field toward their homes.

Ignoring the cautious wisdom of the Banana Cream Pie Paradox, Tippy's reckless journey back through time would end up making one small, seemingly insignificant change. And this one teeny, tiny, itsy-bitsy change would eventually destroy all hopes for the future of our civilization.

As much as I hate to do it, let's go back to the darkened hallway of that fateful, stormy night and find out what *REALLY* happened.

The four distressed delinquents then tumbled down the stairs and shoved their way through the back door of the school. As they ran across the football field toward their homes, something about Kipper and his friends changed forever. They would never again be the same despicable bullies they once were.

CHAPTER 31
THE TERRIBLE, SAD, INCREDIBLY HORRIFYING ENDING

Suddenly, out of nowhere, a ball of blue lightning appeared in front of them. It grew bigger and bigger until it exploded in a blinding flash.

And there, where the ball of lightning had
been, stood a giant pair of robotic pants.

"Boy, that was a close one," said Tippy from inside the depths of his giant Robo-Pants. "Captain Underpants is a lot stronger than I thought!"

Tippy unzipped the zipper of his time-traveling trousers and looked out at the world of five years ago. He saw the raging thunderstorm and the four sixth graders who stood trembling beneath his giant, robotic feet.

"Hey," shouted Tippy. "What's wrong with you kids? You look like you've just seen a ghost!"

"IT'S—IT'S—IT'S THE H-H-HAUNTED P-P-P-PANTS OF W-W-WEDGIE M-M-M-MAGEE!" screamed Finkstein, pointing up at Tippy's gigantic, darkened silhouette. Kipper and his buddies screamed so loud and so high, only dogs could hear them.

What happened next is what psychologists commonly refer to as "Going Cuckoo for Cocoa Puffs." The four sixth graders fell to their knees, shaking, twitching, and uttering complete nonsense as their fragile, eggshell minds began to shatter.

"B-B-Bubba bobba hob-hobba-hobba wah-wah!" cried Kipper, as he frantically slapped himself in the face again and again.

Bugg tore off his clothes and began dancing the hula while singing "I'm a Little Teapot" as loudly as he could.

Loogie started digging a hole in the ground with his teeth, gobbling up enormous fistfuls of dirt and worms. And poor Finkstein just laughed maniacally, happily banging his head into the grass over and over and over and over and over.

LEFT HAND HERE

BULLIES GO
BANANAS!

RIGHT
THUMB
HERE

RIGHT
INDEX
FINGER
HERE

284

BULLIES GO BANANAS!

"Boy," said Tippy, "kids sure were weird five years ago." He quickly reset the controllers of his Tinkle-Time Travelometer to "Four Years in da Future" and pressed the "Away We Go!" button.

Suddenly, giant sparks of blue lightning shot out from the Robo-Pants. Several special-effects-filled moments later, a blinding flash lit up the sky, and Tippy and his Robo-Pants disappeared.

The next day, the four troubled sixth graders were admitted to the Piqua Valley Home for the Reality-Challenged. An investigation into their mental breakdowns led police straight to Mr. Krupp, whose bruised and battered body made everyone VERY suspicious. The cops naturally assumed that Mr. Krupp was somehow behind all of this insanity.

Although no formal charges were filed against Mr. Krupp, everyone blamed him anyway. Mr. Krupp got fired a few weeks later, and he never worked as an elementary school principal again.

CHAPTER 32
FOUR YEARS LATER . . .

Four years later, a giant sphere of blue lightning appeared on what used to be an elementary school football field. Soon, the sphere exploded in a blinding flash of light, leaving Tippy and his gigantic Robo-Pants behind.

Tippy peeked out of the zipper and discovered that Earth had been destroyed.

He crawled out of his giant Robo-Pants and shuffled through the shattered city, inspecting the chaos. All around him, the landscape was littered with massive moon rocks, skeletal skyscrapers, and torn-up toilets.

"What the heck happened here?" Tippy cried.

When the morning sun rose above the horizon, Tippy finally saw a sign of life. A little preschooler was walking up a burning boulevard with his mother.

"Hey, kid," yelled Tippy. "What happened here? How did Earth get destroyed?"

"Well," said the little boy, "a few weeks ago, some guy in a diaper blew up the moon and tried to take over the world. But a week later, a bunch of Talking Toilets attacked the city and ate him up. Then, a week after that, a spaceship landed on top of the elementary school, and all the kids got turned into giant evil zombie nerds!"

"I sure wish you would stop obsessing over such foolish nonsense," the boy's mother said.

"But what about Captain Underpants?" asked Tippy.

"Who's that?" said the boy.

"He's that fat, bald superhero," said Tippy. "You know, the guy with the underwear and the red cape? What happened to him?"

"I've never seen anyone like that," said the little boy.

Suddenly, Tippy realized what a terrible mistake he had made. Somehow he'd changed things in the past, which had resulted in the destruction of both Captain Underpants *AND* Earth.

"I must go back and undo what I did," cried Tippy. "I must go back in time to SAVE Captain Underpants!

"Quickly, little boy," screamed Tippy, "tell me everything you know about these zombie nerds who have taken over the world!"

"Well," said the little boy, "they're really strong—and they're really powerful!"

"Yes, yes," said Tippy. "What *else* are they?"

"They're right behind you," said the boy.

Tippy turned and looked up. There, standing behind him, were two of the biggest, evilest-looking zombie nerds anyone had ever seen.

One of the zombie nerds raised his foot above Tippy's head.

"NOOOOO!" screamed Tippy. "You can't kill me! I'm the only chance this world has of ever returning to normal!"

CHAPTER 33
TO MAKE A LONG STORY SHORT

SPLAT!!!

CHAPTER 34
THE END (OF THE WORLD AS WE KNOW IT)

When the horrible zombie nerd raised his foot again, all that remained was a red squishy stain.

And that, dear readers, is the unfortunate end of the Captain Underpants saga.

Dr. Diaper blew up the moon, the Talking Toilets attacked, and zombie nerds took over Earth. Captain Underpants wasn't there to save the world, because Mr. Krupp wasn't there to get hypnotized by George and Harold.

All of the epic adventures we've come to know and love never actually happened. And now, the only chance of making things right again has just been obliterated.

It is with great sadness that I must tell you: This is the final chapter of the last Captain Underpants epic novel. There will be no more Captain Underpants adventures.

Just kidding, there will be more.
Trust me.

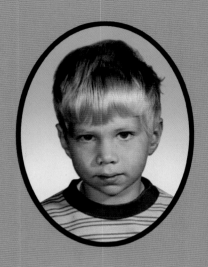

ABOUT THE
AUTHOR-ILLUSTRATOR

When Dav Pilkey was a kid, he was diagnosed with ADHD and dyslexia. Dav was so disruptive in class that his teachers made him sit out in the hall every day. Luckily, Dav loved to draw and make up stories. He spent his time in the hallway creating his own original comic books.

In the second grade, Dav Pilkey made a comic book about a superhero named Captain Underpants. Since then, he has been creating books that explore fun, positive themes and inspire readers everywhere.